Sandcastles and Secrets
A Nanny Blu Cozy Mystery

Summer in Diamond Bay
Book 2

By

Maci Grant

TABLE OF CONTENTS

CHAPTER 1

"Oh, it's so sticky!" Joey sighed and shook his hand right in front of Blu's face.

Blu ducked away from his Popsicle-juice-covered fingers and handed him a napkin. "If you would eat it a bit faster it wouldn't melt all over you, Joey."

"But it's too cold to eat fast!" Joey frowned.

Blu looked at his sun-reddened cheeks and his drooping eyelids. The Popsicle wasn't the problem. Joey was tired.

Over the past few days summer had kicked into high gear. With all of the kids' summer activities they spent just about all of their free time on Diamond Bay's beach. From sunup until sundown, the kids were active and having a blast, but by the end of the day they were tired—especially Joey, who didn't get a nap in the middle of the day like Marley still did.

Marley stumbled backward a few steps. She couldn't see where she was going because she had the Popsicle tipped upside down in her mouth and her head tilted back as far as it could go.

"Marley! Careful!" Blu guided her away from the statue she was about to bump into.

The patio off the back of the beach house was one of Blu's favorite places to be. As she gazed out at the waves the last of the sunlight trickled across their surfaces. She took a deep breath of the sea air and let the fact that this was her life sink in. Just as she drifted off in her mind, a shrill voice snapped her back to the present moment.

"Hi, kiddos!" Maddie jogged up to the patio with a huge smile on her face.

Blu couldn't help but smile back. Maddie was her best friend and always had a way of being loud, even when her mouth was closed. Her presence was vibrant, attention-grabbing, and more than a little demanding.

"Hey, Maddie, how did your day go?" Blu stood up and gave her a quick hug.

"It was fine, but really, how many times can you go to the aquarium? We're at the beach, right?" She laughed. "Anyway, I stopped in town on the way home and I just wanted to let you guys know that the Beach Bum is hosting a sandcastle competition. It's open to everyone— you just have to go down there to sign up."

"Oh, can we sign up Blu, can we, please?" Joey's pout turned into excitement as he met her eyes. "It'll be so much fun! Please say yes?"

"Yes, of course we can." Blu smiled. "I'm glad to see

you excited about something, Joey."

"Excited isn't the word! I'm going to go draw up plans!"

"Oh, he's so cute." Maddie shook her head as Joey disappeared into the house. "I have to say, I'm not really looking forward to it. But the kids talked me into it, so we'll be doing it too."

"Give it a chance, you might have fun."

Blu reached out to untangle a few strands of Marley's hair.

"Honey, with what I pay for these nails..." Maddie displayed her fingernails for Blu to see. The coloring and shading resembled the waves on the horizon.

"They *are* beautiful, but it is the summer." Blu smiled at her.

"Yup, and my kids are older—they can play by themselves." Maddie winked at her. "I have to go. I have a date!"

"Another one? Same guy?"

"Different guy. Wish me luck!"

"Good luck." Blu smiled.

Maddie rushed off looking quite excited. Blu was excited for her. They both worked as nannies, and it was hard to remember sometimes that they were adults. Maddie needed a fun night out. Blu, on the other hand, was content to tug Marley inside for a game of Go Fish.

As they started the card game, Blu's mind returned to thoughts about the sandcastle contest. Since it would take place on the sand behind the Beach Bum, she knew that there was a good chance of running into AJ. The bartender was someone she'd recently met, and though she wasn't really interested in romance, his presence had a strange impact on her. No matter how she tried to shake it, he seemed quite familiar to her.

"Blu, do you have this one?" Marley waved a card in front of Blu's face.

Blu blinked and laughed. "Sorry, sweetie. I don't have it. Go fish!"

"Oh!" Marley sighed with all the drama that a four-year-old could muster and reached into the pool of cards in the middle of the table.

"Don't worry, maybe you'll get what you want." Blu smiled.

"I did, I did. I win!" Marley hopped up and down as she waved the card through the air.

"Good job! Now it's time to go get those teeth brushed!"

CHAPTER 2

Blu plodded through the evening routine with the kids.

Just as she'd gotten them settled into bed, Rachel arrived home from her dinner out with friends. She joined Blu in Marley's bedroom.

"Oh, don't you look tuckered out?" Rachel smiled as she leaned down and planted a kiss on Marley's forehead. "Good night. I love you. Make sure you have good dreams."

"I will, Mommy. I'm going to dream about sandcastles!"

"Lovely!"

"We're entering a sandcastle competition," Blu explained as they left Marley's room.

Rachel stuck her head into Joey's room. "I see that flashlight, young man!"

Blu covered her mouth to hide a laugh. Since the start of summer Joey had decided that he had to read a comic book before bed every night.

"Aw, mom!" Joey whined.

"Joey, we have to get up early, remember?" Blu called out.

"Alright."

She heard the flashlight hit the floor.

"I love that he's so into those comic books." Rachel closed the door to his room. "Sometimes I think kids are smarter than us grown-ups. They know how to enjoy their time."

"Did you have a nice time at dinner?"

"What's nice about expensive drinks and stuffy conversation?" Rachel shrugged. "I guess it's enjoyable once in a while, but only just once in a while, if you know what I mean." She glanced at Blu. "Sometimes I wonder if anyone ever has a real conversation any more."

Blu smiled as she met her employer's eyes. "I'm sure they do now and then."

"I'd like more now than then."

"I know what you mean." Blu grinned. "I hope that you had some fun though."

"The food was good." Rachel nodded and pulled off her heels. "So tell me more about this contest. Is it tomorrow?"

"We're going to enter the beginner's class. I think the competition is at the end of the week on Saturday morning."

"Oh, perfect. Marshall should be here for that."

"Great!" Blu glanced at her watch. "I'd better get to

bed too or I'm not going to be very chipper in the morning."

"That seems impossible, Blu."

Blu glanced over at her. "What does?"

"You being anything but chipper. You always seem so happy."

Blu was a bit surprised by the wistful tone in Rachel's voice. "I guess I am—no complaints." Blu smiled.

"Don't ever lose that, Blu. One day you're annoyed, and the next day you don't know how the world got so gray." She sighed and wandered off down the hall.

Blu stared after her for some time. It was hard to see Rachel having such a tough time. She'd noticed her employer's moods getting darker. At first she'd written it off to the shift from the school year into summer, but the more time that passed the worse it seemed to get. She made a promise to herself that she would try to sit down with Rachel and have a real conversation with her about it. She tried not to get too personal with her employers, but she also wasn't going to turn a blind eye to what looked like depression.

As she brushed her teeth and combed her hair she thought about what might be bothering Rachel. Her husband Marshall's new position at work demanded a lot more travel, and though Rachel had a passion for a few things, her main focus was on charity work and being the wife of a wealthy businessman. She had to be available at a moment's notice for dinner with clients, for trips to different states and even countries. To most, her life might seem wonderful, but Blu knew that it wasn't without its stress.

She sprawled out on her bed with a sense of determination to make the next day a memorable one. Maybe Saturday would be the perfect day for the entire family to reconnect.

When Blu woke up the next morning, it was not to her alarm, or to the sun poking its way through the curtains. She awoke to two children who stood impatiently in front of her bed.

"I think she's awake," Joey whispered to Marley.

"Is she snoring?" Marley squinted at Blu. "If she's snoring, she's sleeping."

"I'm not snoring." Blu raised an eyebrow and grinned at both of them. "I guess you want an early start this morning, hm?"

"I can't wait!" Joey grinned.

"Well, you'll have to wait long enough to eat some oatmeal, okay?" Blu pulled herself out of bed. "Why don't you two go ahead and get dressed so we'll be ready to go when breakfast is over."

"Alright!" Joey grabbed Marley's hand. "Let's go, Marley. The faster we get ready, the faster we'll be at the beach!"

Blu smiled to herself. It was easy for the beach to get

old as a summer activity for the kids, but the idea of being in the contest had rejuvenated their passion for the sand and the waves.

As she dressed and then prepared breakfast, her thoughts turned to who she might run into on the beach. It would be early in the morning so the chances of seeing AJ were slim, but she was pretty sure that Maddie would be there.

Once the kids had eaten their breakfast, the three headed out for the class. When they arrived the other students attending the class were arriving as well.

"Morning, Blu." Maddie plodded up behind them. "I mean, this is really early. What were they thinking?"

"You think this is early? Joey and Marley were in my room by six this morning!"

"Oh boy." Maddie laughed. "I guess they're excited."

"Yes, they are."

"I'm excited to read my new book." Maddie held up a paperback.

"Oh, is it good?"

"So far so good. Let's just say that I'm willing to find out if it gets better."

CHAPTER 3

There was an assortment of chairs set out for people to choose from. Maddie took up residence on one closest to the water and popped open her book. She clearly had no interest in participating in the class.

Joey and Marley, on the other hand, were quite excited to dig right in. They started plowing shovels and pails into the sand before the instructor had even walked over.

"Careful now, don't get sand in your brother's eyes." Blu folded her arms and rested back on her heels as she watched the two children play. It was interesting to her to see how much enthusiasm they had for a simple activity.

A woman walked over to the group. She wore a whistle around her neck and had her black hair piled up high on the top of her head in a ponytail wrapped into a bun.

"Good morning, junior builders. I'm so glad that you're all here."

Blu smiled at her. She seemed friendly enough and nearly as enthusiastic as the kids (along with a handful of adults) who awaited instruction.

"We're going to go ahead and get started. So if everyone can just look up here at me for a minute, I want to tell you a little bit about myself. My name is Sunny and I'm employed by the Castles Contest Group. So wherever the contest goes, I go too." She smiled brightly. "I've been doing this for a few years now and I'd like to explain the rules to you.

"Now, one of the best parts of the competition is our juniors group. Many of the people in our juniors groups are children. Some are adults that are beginners. We have a few rules for the juniors group. The first and most important rule is to be respectful of one another's creations. It can be very tempting when you see a big pile of sand to want to stomp all through it, but please don't do that. Everyone works very hard on their castles, and no one wants them to be destroyed.

"On the last day of the contest after the winners have been selected we have a stomping party. Then, and only then, everyone will get a chance to plow down the castles. But until then, it's important to stay out of each other's areas.

"If you want to work in teams, that's fine. Some of our more experienced competitors take this contest very seriously and you'll notice a few of them setting up now for the contest tomorrow. It's very important that you don't enter their roped-off areas, as they are part of the expert group, and their castles are very delicate. Okay?"

She looked among the faces of all of the members of the class.

"Now if you would like to discuss your ideas, that's fine, but remember no one has any bad ideas. Also, it's best that we not create anything that is too offensive. Before you enter the contest you will submit your ideas for approval. Once you have approval, you can start building at six in the morning. You can have the entire week to work on your castle. So if you build one and change your mind, you can always start over.

"Keep in mind that the experts in the competition do not have this option. They can work in their areas and prepare supplies but may not start building until the morning of the contest. If you have any questions I'm always here and ready to answer. The most important rule is to have fun!"

Joey cheered. "I can't wait! I'm going to make a pirate's castle!"

"Don't be dumb, pirates have boats!" Marley stuck out her tongue. "Only princesses have castles. I'm going to make a princess castle!"

"Pirates can have castles too!"

"Remember, kids, no idea is a bad idea!" Sunny smiled.

"See!" Joy put his hands on his hips.

"Just watch out for the areas that the experts are working in, please." Sunny pointed toward three sections on the beach.

Blu looked over in the direction that Sunny pointed. There were three people setting up in different areas of the sand. Each one had their own roped-off section.

One man was on his hands and knees in the sand. He had a strange comb as long as a ruler. He pulled it through the sand with slow deliberate movements.

In the next section, a woman sat in a yoga pose with sand coating her from knees to folded feet. She had her eyes closed and looked very serene.

The third competitor was dressed in a very strange robe. It was long enough to drag across the sand and it was formed of multiple colors that reminded Blu of the sunset. On top of his head was a cone shaped hat. A bright purple feather stuck out of the top of his hat. He was odd, to say the least, but seemed to be very passionate about what he was doing.

Blu was relieved that she only had to deal with the juniors and not the experts.

As the instructor walked the beginners through the process of dampening sand, stacking blocks, and even tips on building moats, Blu found it impossible to look away from the experts. The thing she noticed the most was that they didn't speak to one another. In fact, they didn't even look at each other. They might as well have been on completely different beaches. All of their focus was on the sand and what they would build.

In her entire life Blu had never considered what it might be like to build a sandcastle for a living. She assumed that if the experts took the contest so seriously, the prize must be quite large. She pulled a chair closer to where Joey and Marley practiced making sand bricks and sat down to watch. But her attention kept drifting back to the man who combed the sand.

CHAPTER 4

"Kirk is very passionate."

Sunny's voice made Blu jump. She hadn't noticed when the woman walked up. "Oh?"

"Yes. He's worked in every contest I've ever been to, since I was just a kid. He creates amazing sculptures, but he is very difficult to work with."

"What about the others?" Blu glanced over at the woman who'd been in the yoga pose and who was now sprawled out across the sand with her face turned up to the sun.

"Bianca." Sunny grinned. "She's new to the contest. She's been doing it for about two years. She's an environmental activist and uses it as a tool to illustrate the plight of sea animals. One year she decorated her sculpture with all kinds of garbage. Some if it even smelled."

"Ugh. Not so pleasant."

"No, but she does have a point. At least she's trying to make a difference—unlike Yale." Sunny gestured toward the third contestant. "I'm not sure what he's trying to do."

"Yale?"

"I don't think that's his real name, but that's what he uses on the contest papers. I'd say he's been in about five contests and each one is stranger than the last. One time he had some strange music playing, and he had a portable spotlight as well as a strobe light. You can imagine how that worked on a sunny beach." She rolled her eyes. "But he makes quite an effort, and I do have to say that every single time his sculpture is a surprise."

"Well, then, I'm looking forward to seeing it."

"Get here early. The beach gets very crowded for the experts' contest. I wish I could say all of the fans come for all of the castles, but these three have followers that travel the country to see them in action."

"Wow." Blu shook her head. "I didn't know that it was that big of a deal."

"It is to them." Sunny shrugged. "I guess that's all that matters."

After Sunny walked off, Blu watched Yale open a plastic container. Inside was an assortment of feathers dyed bright orange, pink, dark purple, and sky blue. As she lost herself in thought about what the feathers might be used for, she neglected her child-watching duties.

"Don't, Joey! That's my sand!" Marley reached for her brother's foot as he tried to run away.

Joey lost his balance and fell forward into the sand.

Blu jumped up to see if he was hurt. Before she could

reach him, Kirk shouted at the tops of his lungs.

"Away from my sand! This is the only warning that you'll get! Understand? You kids need to stay out of my area!"

"Sorry, I fell!" Joey jumped up and backed away from the furious man.

Blu wrapped an arm around Joey. "He didn't mean to. It was an accident."

"He needs to be more careful! This isn't a game. This is my life!"

Blu could feel Joey tremble against her. Her protective nature threatened to spill over in the form of angry words, but she reminded herself that she had to set a good example for the kids.

"I'm very sorry that he disturbed you, sir. I'll make sure that they play a little farther away."

"You do that." He turned back to his sand.

"I'm sorry, Blu." Joey sniffled.

"It's alright, honey. Some people just take things more seriously than others. Just do your best to stay away from his area. Marley, no tripping your brother."

Marley nodded and dug her shovel into the sand again. As she tried to make a big pile of sand, some of it was flung off her shovel. It landed in little piles inside the roped-off area that belonged to Kirk.

"No! No! No!" Kirk shouted. His face was beet red as he turned to look at Marley.

Blu stepped between them. "Calm down, it's just a

little sand. What is it really going to hurt?"

"I'm preparing my sand for the contest. It takes me days to get the balance perfect. Every drop of ungroomed sand that invades my perfect canvas forces me to start all over again."

"Kirk, they're just kids." Yale waved a feather at him. "Stop worrying so much. You're going to lose anyway."

"You shut your mouth. Yale!"

"Stop it, please!" Bianca put her hands over her ears. "I can't work in this chaos and disharmony! Now I'll have to start all over again to cleanse the energy of my area!"

"Maybe you should work on cleansing yourself first, or at least put your arms down!" Kirk snarled.

"Oh, my." Blu grabbed Joey's hand. "Let's go get a snow cone, kids!"

"But we're building!" Marley stamped a flip-flop.

"Marley, we're going to come back tomorrow, but I think it's best if we leave right now."

Blu bit into the tip of her tongue to keep from saying more than that. The last thing that she wanted to do was get into an argument in front of the kids. She tended to be mild-mannered, but when it came to protecting small children she could be quite vicious.

She hurried the children away from the beach and toward the parking lot beside the Beach Bum.

CHAPTER 5

Blu was so annoyed that she kept her eyes on the ground beneath her feet. When she heard a car door slam shut, she jumped and looked up to see AJ beside his jeep.

"Morning, kids. Having fun?" AJ smiled at Joey and Marley.

Marley shook her head and pointed at Blu.

AJ frowned. "Blu? What's wrong?"

"I don't want to talk about it." Blu tightened her grip on Joey's hand and tried to brush past AJ.

"Wait a minute."

Blu tensed when she felt AJ's touch on her arm. As quick as he touched her, he pulled his hand back. "Something happened? What's the problem?"

"There's a mean guy on the beach!" Joey muttered.

"A mean guy? Who?" AJ narrowed his eyes. "Is someone bothering you three?"

"It's nothing like that, AJ." Blu avoided looking at him. "It's one of the expert competitors. He's just a bit picky about his sand. He was yelling at a few of the kids,

Joey and Marley included."

"Who is it? I'll throw him off of the beach right this second." His expression darkened as he turned toward the beach.

Blu took a slight step back. She was surprised that AJ was so determined to stand up for them all. Or was it just the kids?

"Wait, AJ, don't. It's not really his fault. I should have been watching the kids better. It seems to me this guy lives for this contest. I wouldn't want him to miss out just because I wasn't doing the best I could to keep the kids out of his hair."

"That's very thoughtful of you." AJ turned back to look at her with a half-smile. "If it were me he'd be swimming with the sharks already."

"Hey, it's everybody's beach, right?" Blu smiled.

"Sure. But if he gives you any more trouble I want you to tell me, understand?" He waited until Blu looked up at him, and then met her eyes. "I mean it. I don't want him bullying you or the kids. Okay?"

Blu tried to hide her smile but it blossomed on her lips before she could. "Thanks, AJ."

"No problem. See you tomorrow." He waved to the kids then walked off toward the beach.

Blu wondered if he was going to have a conversation with Kirk after all. She didn't think it would be so terrible if he did.

Once she had the kids settled with snow cones Blu

sent a text to Maddie.

Are you still at the beach?

Maddie texted right back.

Leaving now. These people are nuts.

Blu invited her to join them for snow cones. She smiled when Maddie agreed. Before Maddie started working as a nanny, Blu was often without a friend during the summer months. It was nice to have someone nearby to spend time with.

A few minutes later Maddie and her charges arrived. Maddie joined Blu at the table while the kids settled in at another table.

"Can you believe that nutcase on the beach?" Maddie shook her head. "He started shouting at me because I brushed some sand off my sandals. I don't even know why they're allowing kids to participate in the contest if the contestants are going to be that crazy."

"I know, I couldn't believe that he was combing the sand." Blu laughed. "I guess that it's important enough to him to be that focused, but they need to realize that kids are part of the equation. I'm sure AJ will say something to him."

"Oh, you're sure?" Maddie leaned close to her. "Just why are you so sure? Hm?"

"Maddie, stop!" Blu rolled her eyes.

"It sounds to me that things between you and AJ are getting rather personal."

"Only you could turn two nearly nonexistent

conversations into some kind of relationship."

"That's how it starts, you know. A conversation here, a chance meeting there, and before you know it, you're married with five kids."

Blu nearly choked on her snow cone. "Now I'm pretty sure that you're the one that's nuts. That will never happen to me."

"You never know. True love often comes out of the blue."

"I might not know about that, but I do know I'm not having five kids!"

"Okay, fair enough. That you might have some control over." She lowered her voice so that Marley and Joey couldn't hear her. "But I sure wouldn't mind having a few with AJ."

"You should ask him out." Blu's eyes widened. "That's a great idea! You guys would be perfect together."

"Uh, I don't think so. I've seen the way that you look at him." Maddie shook her head. "In my mind, that man is taken."

"Wait a minute! I don't look at him in any special way. If you see something, it's probably because he reminds me of someone. I just can't place who. Anyway, he's not taken. He's the opposite of taken. I'd love to see you happy with someone, and AJ seems like a great guy."

"So, why wouldn't *you* ask him out?" Maddie frowned.

"We've talked about this. I like the way my life is right now. I went through that dating and looking for a husband phase. Now I'm rather settled into the idea of being free to live my life how I choose. Is that really so wrong?" Blu finished her snow cone.

"Maybe not wrong, but I don't know if I believe you."

"Believe me or not, but if you don't go after AJ I can guarantee you that one of these young nannies will."

"Ouch, good point." Maddie wiggled her eyebrows. "He's not going to be on the market long."

"Blu, can I have another?" Marley smiled at her with bright blue teeth.

"Oh, no, I think we better get you home to brush your teeth."

"Oh, yes!" Maddie laughed. "We'll see you guys tomorrow?"

"Absolutely." Blu stood up and rounded up the kids. "Hopefully things will be calmer."

"Hopefully AJ will be there to supervise." Maddie winked at her.

Blu only laughed as she herded the kids out the door.

CHAPTER 6

On the way to the car Marley started to cry.

"Marley, what's wrong?" Blu looked down at her.

"I left my favorite pail at the beach!"

"Are you sure?" Blu frowned. "I thought I cleaned everything up." She sighed as she realized that she'd been in such a rush, she might have overlooked the pail.

"I know I did. It's there. Someone will take it!" Big tears rolled down Marley's cheeks.

"Oh, sweetie, we can get it tomorrow, can't we? We'll be back there in the morning."

"Someone will take it!" Marley wailed.

"Alright, alright. Let's go back to the beach. I'm sure it will still be there."

She hustled the kids into the car and drove back to the beach. Most of the kids had cleared the area, but the experts were still there.

"Stay out of their way." Blu did her best to steer the kids away from the roped-off sand. She knew that the more she tried to keep them away, the more they would want to wander over there, but she hoped that she could find the pail before that happened.

The pail was not in sight at first. Blu scanned the beach area that they'd occupied earlier.

As she looked over the beach she noticed a woman who stood several feet away from where the experts were working on their sand. She wore a huge floppy sunhat, big sunglasses, and a flowing sundress. She reminded Blu of a cross between a movie star and a spy. The woman stared, not at the beautiful water, but at the three experts working on their sand sculptures.

Blu spotted the pail not far from where the woman stood. She hurried toward it. As Blu approached, the woman turned and walked away in the other direction.

"There it is!" Marley barreled past Blu and scooped up the bucket, which just happened to contain a large amount of cool water that splashed all over Blu's shins and feet.

Blu yelped with surprise. "Marley!"

"Sorry." Marley giggled.

"Quiet, please!" Bianca shrieked. "I'm trying to chant!"

"That's it. We're done with the beach today, kids." Blu shook her head and escorted the kids back to the car.

All that afternoon the kids drew pictures of what they might create in the sand. Blu enjoyed listening to them banter back and forth about their ideas and other sculptures that they'd seen. Maybe the experts were difficult to deal with, but the kids were still having a lot of fun.

"How did it go this morning?" Rachel walked in with a pile of mail in her hand.

"It was good." Blu nodded. "The contest should be interesting."

"Great. Marshall said he'll definitely be here, so I'm excited. But it's probably best not to mention it to the children until we know for sure."

"I understand."

"How about you, Blu? Want the night off? I'm home and would love to snuggle up with the kids and a movie."

"Are you sure?"

"Absolutely. Any time I can get with them makes me happy. Besides, this is your summer too. I want you to have the chance to get out and have some fun. I hear there's a bonfire down on the beach tonight."

"Oh." Blu swallowed hard. She couldn't imagine trying to blend in with all of the young nannies and locals that would be there. "Thanks, Rachel."

"You really should go. I know it may seem like you have all the time in the world now, but trust me when I tell you that time is fleeting."

Blu nodded and smiled at Rachel. It was kind of her to be concerned. But Blu still didn't think that she would survive the bonfire.

After Rachel and the kids were curled up on the

couch, Blu texted Maddie to see if she was going to the bonfire.

Will be there, and so will AJ!

Blu frowned. That was even more reason not to go.

But maybe Rachel was right. Summer only lasted so long, and Blu would soon be back to juggling homework, extracurricular activities, and play dates. It was a life she loved, but it often didn't leave her a lot of free time for herself. Of course a bonfire was not her idea of fun. Still, she thought it would be best to get out of the house as Rachel requested.

It wasn't always easy living with another adult in the house, even if she was paid to be there. At least Maddie would be at the bonfire, which meant she was bound to have a little fun.

As she left the house she actually experienced a brief surge of excitement. The moon was on the rise, the weather was a perfect balmy temperature, and she could already smell the bonfire in the air.

She made her way to the edge of the beach. In the flicker of the firelight she could see several familiar faces. None of them were Maddie.

Blu lingered by the entrance of the beach. She wasn't sure if she wanted to break into the party without knowing if Maddie was there. She pulled out her phone and dialed Maddie's number. As she waited for her to answer, she heard a cell phone ring nearby. She turned in the direction of the sound and found Maddie walking toward her—with her arm linked through AJ's.

Blu lowered her eyes, as for a split second an embarrassing amount of jealousy rushed through her. What was that? She couldn't even think it through, as Maddie slung her arm through Blu's.

"Ready for some fun?"

"I think so." Blu smiled.

"It's good to see you, Blu." AJ tipped his head toward her. "Maddie found me restocking the bar and insisted that I join in on the fun."

"She has a knack for that." Blu laughed. All traces of jealousy disappeared as fast as the fire snapped out a few embers.

"There are some beers in the cooler and I think there are some bottles of wine floating around too."

"Alcohol on the beach?" Blu raised an eyebrow.

"It's a party, Blu, relax." Maddie gave her arm a squeeze. "I'll get us some drinks, you two find us a spot near the fire."

"Will do." AJ nodded as Maddie walked away.

CHAPTER 7

Blu glanced over at the clear blue water. She clasped her hands behind her back and tried not to pay attention to the fact that AJ was right beside her.

"We don't normally allow it, but with the sandcastle competition there's a lot of people that are in from out of town—it's just one night." AJ shrugged. "What's a little bending of the rules?"

"You mean breaking the law?" Blu looked over at him. "I guess that's not a big deal to you, since the law will not come down on you, huh?"

"Wow, wait a minute. Slow down." He laughed. "I requested and received permission from the police chief—like anyone else could. He offered to provide added security for the event, just like he would for anyone, Blu."

Blu lowered her eyes. "I'm sorry. I didn't realize."

"No, you just assumed I was a criminal." He leaned a little closer to her. "Or at the very least not a very good bartender."

"I really didn't mean that." Blu sighed. "I guess I'm

used to dealing with kids."

"So now I'm a kid?" AJ crossed his arms.

Blu looked up at him with a frown.

"No, that's not what I meant at all."

She noticed that AJ's lips seemed to be quivering. It certainly wasn't cold on the beach. Had she offended him so much that he was about to cry? Just when she was getting ready to apologize again, AJ broke out laughing.

"I'm sorry. Man, you're always so serious. I just wanted to joke around a bit with you—thought maybe I could make you smile."

"That wasn't very nice." She grinned.

"But it worked."

"Well, if it's fun you're looking for, Maddie is the right girl for you."

"Maddie? Sure she seems like fun." AJ shrugged and shoved his hands into his pockets.

"She's very fun. She always keeps me laughing." Blu walked toward the fire with AJ a few steps behind.

"Here you go." Maddie joined them at the fire. She handed them each a bottle of beer and opened one for herself.

Blu pretended to take a sip. She wasn't much for drinking, especially in public places. But she didn't mind blending in.

"Thanks."

"Thanks a lot, Maddie." AJ took a swig of his beer and squinted at the firelight. "It's a beautiful night."

"You know what it's perfect for?" Blu smiled.

"What?" AJ looked over at her.

"A nice long walk on the beach. Don't you think, AJ?"

"Yes, it is." He stepped closer to her. "Is that an invitation?"

"It's more like a suggestion. I'm a bit too tired for walking, but I'm sure Maddie would be up for it."

"Oh?" AJ blinked. He looked over at Maddie. "Is that right?"

"Sure, I'd love to take a walk." Maddie grinned.

As they walked off together Blu felt a sense of relief. No matter how hard she tried to shake it, she couldn't ignore the feeling that AJ felt familiar to her. It was like he was a long-lost friend.

By the time Maddie and AJ returned from their walk, the fire had died down and Blu had had her fill of small talk.

"Well, this was fun. I think I'm going to head home."

"Already?" Maddie pouted.

"I know, I know. But I've got the class early in the morning, and to be honest, I'm really tired."

"I'll walk you to your car." AJ unwound his arm from Maddie's.

"Oh, actually I didn't drive. I walked."

"Then I'll walk you to your house." AJ tilted his head toward the dark street. "It's a bit late to walk home alone."

"I think I'll be fine." Blu smiled.

"I insist."

"You insist?"

"Blu, it's really not a bad idea." Maddie finished her beer. "There are people drinking on the beach. There may be people driving drunk. What's a little company hurt? Right, AJ?"

"That's right." He nodded.

"Alright, you can walk me to the end of the block. Will that be safe enough?"

"I suppose it will have to do."

Blu gave Maddie a quick hug, then she and AJ began to walk across the beach to the parking lot.

She tried to think of something—anything—to say, but AJ's presence seemed to be making any clear thoughts impossible. Why?

"Thanks for the escort, AJ."

"It's my pleasure." They reached the other side of the parking lot. "I'm looking forward to seeing Joey and Marley's sculptures."

"Me too. They're really excited about it." Blu glanced over at him. "I can take it from here. I'm sure that Maddie is waiting to share another drink with you."

AJ paused and looked over at her with a quirked eyebrow. "Why do you keep mentioning Maddie?"

"Do I?" Blu smiled in what she hoped was an innocent way.

AJ's expression remained stiff with his jaw locked. He

drew his hands out of his pockets and folded his arms. "You do. You keep encouraging me to spend time with her."

"Is there something wrong with that? Maddie's an amazing woman—and she's fun. Why wouldn't you want to spend time with her?" Blu's words were muddled by her own confusion.

"I'm sure that Maddie is amazing. I'm sure that there is nothing wrong with her. But no, I don't have any interest in spending time with her."

"Oh." Blu blinked. His tone was rather cold. She hoped that Maddie hadn't gotten too invested in the idea of dating him. "I'm sorry. I guess I just thought—you're single, she's single, and—well, it seemed like a good match."

"Did it?" He raised an eyebrow and unfolded his arms. As his arms fell back to his sides he took a single step in her direction.

The movement caused Blu's cheeks to flush for a reason she couldn't explain.

"Yes, otherwise, I wouldn't have encouraged it. I'm sorry, I guess I was mistaken. Maybe you're already seeing someone?"

"No. No one." His posture relaxed. "I'm a little selective about who I spend my time with. You know, the summer crowd, groupies or romantics, not much in between."

"I guess." Blu frowned. "I should get going. It's late."

"Which is why I should walk you."

"But I thought you were selective about who you spend your time with?" Blu grinned. Her words were an attempt to lighten the mood that had become strained between them.

AJ didn't crack a smile. Instead he slid his hands back into his pockets and rocked forward some on his toes.

"I am." He met her eyes. "I'd be more than happy to walk you home, Blu."

CHAPTER 8

Blu stared at AJ as her mind caught up with their conversation. Was it possible that he was trying to indicate that he wanted to spend time with her? She was so rusty when it came to the dating game that she couldn't be confident in her ability to read the situation. She felt her cheeks growing warm as she looked away from him.

"Like I said, I'm fine to walk home. But I appreciate the offer."

"Alright then." He looked like he was about to say more, but then he turned and walked away without another word.

Blu stared after him for a moment. She still wasn't clear on what had just happened between them. AJ didn't seem angry, or disappointed that she'd declined his offer, so maybe he really was just being polite?

She shook her head to clear her thoughts. She turned and started toward the beach house. As she reached the end of the driveway it occurred to her that she could have just said yes and shared a nice walk with someone who seemed to be a nice guy, despite her attempts to find clues that contradicted that. So what was it about AJ that made her so hesitant to be alone with him?

Over the next few days Blu and the kids showed up every morning to work on their castles. Each morning the three experts were there as well. Blu didn't see AJ again, but she did notice that Maddie had moved on to one of the newer contestants in the sand sculpture contest, which made her feel oddly relieved.

By the time they left the beach each day, Marley and Joey always changed their minds about their sandcastles. Blu enjoyed witnessing their creative sides.

She was fairly certain that she'd offended AJ but she tried no to think about it.

The closer the contest got, the more uptight Rachel became. She made sure everything was spotless, that Marshall's favorite meal was ready to cook, and it seemed that she couldn't help but mention his name every five minutes. Blu thought it was adorable, but she also hoped that Rachel wouldn't end up disappointed.

On the Friday before the contest Blu was just about beached out. Her flip-flops were broken, her sunscreen was almost gone, and Maddie was on her third book. The tension between the experts had increased quite a bit. There was excitement as well as fear in the air.

As Blu gathered the kids to leave the beach, she nearly tripped over someone's foot. She righted herself and looked up into an oversized pair of sunglasses.

"Oh, excuse me, I'm sorry."

"It's my fault." The woman moved to the side. "I was just leaving."

"So are we—a little too much sun today." Blu looked at the woman curiously. She had seen her at the beach every morning throughout the week. "Are you entered in the contest?"

"Oh, no. No. I'm just a fan." She smiled and adjusted her hat. "Oops, I must have forgotten my towel. I better go back and get it." She hurried past Blu and went a bit further down the beach.

Blu squinted. She was sure that the woman hadn't had a towel the entire time. She shook her head and turned back to the kids.

"Alright, you two, let's get you home, bathed, fed, and off and into bed so that you can be ready early in the morning for the contest."

"We're going to win!" Joey jumped up and down.

"Well, Joey, the important thing is to have a good time, right?"

"Sure." Joey rushed ahead of Blu toward the parking lot. "But winning is fun too!"

Blu laughed and raced to catch up with him.

The morning of the contest, Blu was as nervous as Rachel. She did her best to keep a cheerful attitude, but she could tell that Rachel was anxious.

As the kids finished their breakfast, Blu checked her watch. Marshall was late. She glanced across the table at Rachel. It was easy to see the tension in her face. The way her jaw was clenched, the furrow of her brow, and the tightness of her lips all blended together to create a strained expression.

"Should I take the kids down to the beach? You and Marshall could meet us there?"

"No." Rachel set her coffee cup down on the table. "We're all going to go as a family. Marshall will be here soon."

"I don't want to miss the competition." Joey handed Blu his plate. "Please, can Blu take us now, Mom?"

Rachel sighed.

"Your Mom is right, Joey," Blu said. "Your dad has been looking forward to this, and I'm sure that he'll want to go to the beach with you. The contest runs all day long."

"Thanks, Blu." Rachel gazed at her coffee. She jumped when her phone buzzed.

When she picked it up, Blu held her breath. She wanted so badly for there to be good news—maybe Marshall was already at the beach, maybe he was right outside the door. But a moment later Rachel's cheeks were red and her lashes drooped.

"His flight was delayed." She tossed the phone down on the table. It landed with a clatter.

Marley gulped down the last bite of her cereal.

"Rachel, I—" Blu tried to think of the right thing to say.

"Just take them, please. Take them down to the beach. I'll meet you there in a little while."

"We can go together."

"No. It's better to take them now. Please. I just want them to have fun."

Blu bit into her lip. She felt awful for Rachel. An ache started in the pit of her stomach. Maybe this was why she didn't have much interest in romance. In all the families she'd worked with she had seen the intimate side of marriage that few others witnessed. She knew that it wasn't always easy. Even with Rachel and Marshall, who adored each other, there were ongoing problems.

She turned toward the kids. "Okay, guys, go get changed, and get your game faces on!"

CHAPTER 9

When Blu arrived at the beach with the kids, it was already packed, just as Sunny had predicted. There were people in the water and many more people lined up in chairs with a good view of the sand where the contestants would be working on their sculptures.

"You two pick out a good spot to start building." Blu sat down in the sand near them. She watched as they shared their toys and set up in the area where they wanted to build their castle. Once she was sure they were getting along well, she looked away from them, toward the area that was roped off for the experts.

She saw that Bianca had lit candles in all four corners of her patch of sand. Yale was mixing some kind of colored powder into his sand. She braced herself as she looked toward Kirk's patch of sand. She was sure that he would be snapping and hollering with the amount of chaos on the beach.

His pristine sand was completely empty. She looked around at the crowded beach, but she didn't see him anywhere. She did notice the woman with the floppy hat and the big sunglasses.

Just as Blu noticed her, the woman walked off the beach toward the Beach Bum. Blu was distracted for a moment as she wondered if AJ was inside.

"Blu, what do you think?" Joey plunked a shell on the top of a triangle of sand that he'd worked hard to build.

"It looks wonderful, Joey."

"I'm making the moat!" Marley swept her shovel through the sand as fast as she could.

Joey brushed off some of the sand that she splatted on his arm. "Could you please keep your moat to yourself?"

Blu smiled at the kids but she was distracted by the empty sand. It was odd to her that Kirk wouldn't be there.

The contest officially began and the two experts that were there set to work. Blu enjoyed watching the meticulous way that they crafted their sculptures. Then she noticed that some of the other competitors began to pull sand from Kirk's space.

At first, it was a shovel here, or a pailful there. Then it seemed to become a free-for-all—with everyone hoping to beat one of the experts at grabbing up the sand from the empty spot. Blu thought it wasn't very fair, but it was clear that Kirk had decided not to attend the contest.

Then she noticed something odd that stuck up out of the sand. Blu stared at the sand. She tried to reason with herself about what it was that she thought she was seeing.

Were they some kind of oddly shaped shells? Maybe a crab of some type? What they looked like, they simply couldn't be. Yet she couldn't look away.

More and more sand was scooped away until there was no mistaking what she'd seen. She opened her mouth to cry out, but before she could someone else screamed. The high-pitched scream carried loudly over the din of the people at the beach—over the laughter of children and the splash of the waves.

Blu jumped up and grabbed Marley into her arms. "Joey, come here." She held out her hand to him.

"But Blu, I'm still working on the castle. I want to see if I can get it to be taller than me."

"I'm sorry, Joey, we have to go."

Blu looked back over at Kirk's section of sand. A crowd formed around it, but Blu was still worried about the children getting a clear view of what was sticking up out of the sand.

"What's going on?" Joey tried to pull his hand away from her, but Blu kept a tight grip on it.

She steered the two children clear of the area and hoped that they didn't hear the screams. Blu was so shaken by what she'd seen that she knew she couldn't drive. Her hands trembled so much that she couldn't think to text.

She led the kids toward the Beach Bum to escape the commotion and keep them away from the truth. The strange objects she'd seen in the sand weren't shells or crabs, they were human toes—attached to human feet, attached to what she assumed was a dead body.

When she pulled open the door to the bar, she noticed it was empty inside. She was relieved that it was at least open.

"Blu, why are we in here?" Marley pouted. "I want to go back to the beach."

"Yeah, Dad is supposed to meet us!" Joey crossed his arms.

"Right now the beach isn't safe for us. We have to wait until the police say it's safe to go back on the sand."

"What police?" Joey peered out the window. Blu pointed out the police cars that were pulling into the parking lot.

"Somebody's in trouble!" Marley sang out.

Blu ruffled her hair and tried to stay calm. Just as she took a deep breath the back door of the bar swung open. AJ stepped in with a large box in his hands.

"Blu, hi there." AJ set the box down on the floor just inside the bar. "You okay?"

"We're just in here to stay out of the way of the police." Blu tilted her head toward the window. "I think there are some things that they just shouldn't see."

"You're right." AJ shot a frown toward the door. "I don't even know what to make of it at this point."

"I don't think that the police do either." Blu crossed her arms as she watched a police officer rope off the area.

AJ cleared his throat. All at once Blu remembered

that AJ's uncle was the police chief. "No offense, AJ. I just think that the situation is so outlandish. Who would do such a thing? In front of children?" She shook her head.

"No one in their right mind, that's for sure." AJ grimaced. "I'm not sure that the contest will go on.

"I'll go check on things. You guys can stay in here as long as you need to." AJ stepped out of the bar.

CHAPTER 10

Blu pulled her phone out and to call Rachel. The phone went straight to voicemail.

"Rachel, there's a problem on the beach. I don't know if you and Marshall are headed here now, but if you are, it's probably better to meet back at the house."

She texted her the same information.

Just when she was about to put her phone back in her pocket, it started to ring.

"Hello?"

"Blu, this is crazy!"

Blu winced when she heard Maddie's voice. "Did the kids see?"

"No, they're out in the water, thankfully."

"Do they know who it is?"

"Yes. It's Kirk—that grumpy guy that was in the contest."

"Kirk?" Blu's eyes widened. "So that's why he didn't show up for today."

"Oh, I'd say he showed up alright. You should see the police officers out here trying to figure out how to get him out of the sand. I thought I was bad when it came to organizing, but these guys have me beat."

"Is the chief there yet?"

"He just arrived. Oh, and of course AJ's here."

"What's AJ doing?"

"Speaking to his uncle. They look like they might be arguing. Oops, I have to go. The police are clearing the beach."

"We're in the Beach Bum, if you want to come over here."

"We're going to head home, I think. I don't want the kids knowing too much about what's going on until I speak to their mother, since—you know, their father being in jail and all—this might bring up some issues for them."

Blu grimaced. "You're right. Let me know if you need any help with anything."

"I will. Call me if you find out anything about Kirk."

"I'm going to find out what I can. I hope they can get to the bottom of this quickly."

"Right now they only seem interested in scooting everyone off the beach. Bye, Blu."

"Bye." Blu hung up the phone. A second later it began to ring again. "Hello?"

"Blu, what's going on? Marshall and I just arrived at the beach and there are a ton of cop cars. Is everyone okay?"

"I guess you didn't get my message. I'll tell you what

happened later. The kids are fine, but the beach is closed for a criminal investigation. Can we meet you two at the house?"

"Yes. Please do."

Blu hung up the phone. "Hey, guys, guess what?" Blu steered them toward the door. "We're going to go right home and see Mom and Dad."

"Dad?" Joey's eyes lit up. "Is he really there?"

"Yes he is, sweetheart, and he can't wait to see you and your sister."

The three walked out to the parking lot amidst a crowd of other people. Blu glanced over her shoulder at the beach. She saw the police tape that roped off a large area. As she reached the car she heard a loud voice.

"Just because he can't win, now we can't compete at all? It's absurd. It's an absolute travesty. How can we be punished because someone decided to give in to homicidal desires? It's just like Kirk to die. He must have known he was about to lose!"

Blu stared with disbelief as Yale walked past with three others following after him. It took a very callous person to be able to speak so dismissively about someone's death. She couldn't imagine what Kirk could have done to Yale to make him so hateful.

She hurried the kids to the car so that they wouldn't hear more than they already had.

"I can't believe they canceled the contest." Joey pouted as he stared out through the car window.

"It's not fair." Marley crossed her arms and kicked the back of Blu's seat.

"It's not anyone's fault. Sometimes things don't go the way we plan. At least you'll still get to spend time with your dad."

"I wanted him to see my sand sculpture." Joey rested his forehead against the window.

"I promise, once the police are done with their investigation, we'll all go out to the beach, then you can show him."

"It won't be the same."

"It might be, if you give it a try."

"It won't be, because by the time they're done, Dad will probably be gone."

Blu pulled into the driveway of the beach house and parked the car. She turned in her seat to look at Joey. "Sweetheart, I know it's hard for you to understand now, but one day you'll see how hard he worked for you and your family."

"I guess." Joey opened his car door.

"Just try to remember that the only place either of your parents would like to be is right here with both of you. But when you grow up, and you have all of the responsibilities of being a grown-up, that's not always possible."

"But you're always with us." Marley smiled.

"That's because I'm lucky." Blu poked Marley's nose with a light touch.

"Let's go in. Your mom and dad are waiting for you. Try to have a good attitude, hm?"

Joey nodded and stepped out of the car.

Blu helped Marley out and the three of them walked up to the front door of the house.

Joey burst through the door and ran right into his father's arms. Marshall swept him up into the air and hugged him close. Blu smiled to herself. Marshall might not always be home, but when he was, he was a very hands-on father. It was something that she admired about him.

"Hey, buddy, I'm so glad to see you." He reached down and scooped up Marley as well.

Rachel laughed as she embraced all three of them.

Blu took the opportunity to slip away and allow them their moment as a family.

CHAPTER 11

Once Blu was in her room her thoughts returned to Kirk. She paced back and forth as she considered the possibilities of what might have happened to him. Around the children she was careful to keep her focus on them, but now all she could think about was the body. It unsettled her that Joey and Marley were playing only feet away from the dead body.

With Yale's behavior fresh in her mind she decided to do a little research on him. Before she could get into it, she needed to check on the kids.

Rachel caught her in the hallway. "Blu, I want to take Marshall and the kids out to that new ice cream place in town. You can come along if you like, but only as a guest."

"Oh, thank you, but if you don't mind, I'd rather stay here. I know the kids are excited to have their time with Marshall, and I have a little bit of reading that I could catch up on."

"Sure, that's fine. What a horrible thing that happened on the beach today. A friend just filled me in."

"Don't worry—Joey and Marley didn't see any of it."

"Oh, I know that. You always take good care of them."

"Enjoy your ice cream."

"Enjoy your book." Rachel winked at her, then walked back toward the living room to join the others.

Blu turned back to her room and closed the door. Without a moment's hesitation she snatched up her computer. She logged in and did a search on Yale. She figured that a man with such a dramatic presence would certainly have an Internet presence.

It didn't take long for her to find it. The first few links were just to sites dedicated to his creative sand sculptures. The next link was to a series of video blogs. Blu clicked on the first one and Yale's voice filled her dark room. She grabbed her headphones and plugged them in.

"So yet again I have to compete against the worthless Kirk. I'm not even sure why they keep letting him into the contest. He does the same type of sculpture every time. It's so boring. He's always complaining about everything—from the content of the sand to the clouds in the sky. Then I have to sit back and watch him win first place over my much more inventive sand art."

"Looks like Yale really had it in for him," she muttered out loud.

She clicked through a few other video blogs. Each one was similar to the last, directly targeting Kirk. Blu thought it was strange that Yale only went after Kirk, not any other competitors. After the callous way he spoke about Kirk's death it was clear that no love was lost between the two. Was it possible that Yale was the one who buried him in the sand?

She glanced at her watch. It was just after noon. The Beach Bum would probably be open. One thing she knew for sure was that AJ played a big part in organizing the sand sculpture contest. He likely knew a bit about Yale, and even Kirk. She decided it was time to find out just how much he did know.

There were only a few cars in the parking lot at the Beach Bum. Not too many locals started drinking so early. As Blu walked toward the door she noticed AJ's jeep parked at the side of the bar. The sight of it inspired a slight smile despite the troubling situation.

She opened the door and was greeted by the scent of cheese fries and fresh coffee. It was an odd combination.

Behind the bar AJ was drying and stacking glasses. He turned around when Blu let in a flood of light by opening the door.

"Back so soon?" He smiled at her.

"I guess I couldn't stay away." She studied him as she settled on a bar stool not far from him. She couldn't help but wonder what it was that he had been arguing about with his uncle.

"A beer?" He started to turn around to retrieve it.

"No thanks. It's a bit early for me."

"That it is, but after a day like today, who couldn't use a drink?"

"Speaking of which, what exactly happened out there on the beach? Do you know anything about it?'

"Probably as much as you know. Kirk was found dead—buried in sand."

"Any idea why?"

"Well, he wasn't exactly everyone's favorite person."

"That's all you've got?" Blu sniffed the air. "How about some of those cheese fries?"

"Alright." AJ walked away from the bar and through the double doors into the kitchen.

As Blu glanced around at the other patrons she noticed the woman with the floppy hat, only she wasn't wearing her sunglasses any more.

CHAPTER 12

Blu stood up and walked toward the small wooden table where the woman sat. The closer she got, the more clearly she could see why she wasn't wearing her sunglasses. Tears streaked the woman's cheeks. She gripped a large glass of beer. There were two empty glasses beside it. That was heavy drinking.

"Hello there, are you okay?" Blu sat down without being invited.

The woman looked across the table at her. She was young, younger even than Blu. For a moment Blu considered that she might be one of the summer nannies.

"I'm fine." She sniffed and then took a swallow of her beer.

"You don't look fine." Blu reached into her purse and pulled out a fresh tissue. "Is this about what happened today?"

"I'd rather not talk about it."

Blu narrowed her eyes. She had seen this woman staring at Kirk many times. "Sometimes talking about it can help you to feel a bit better."

"I don't think it will in this case."

"Look, I'm not going to pretend that I didn't notice you on the beach. It seemed to me that you were quite interested in Kirk."

The woman fiddled with the tissue, but didn't say a word.

Blu decided to continue with her questions. "Are you a fan of his?"

"What does it matter?"

"I'm Blu." Blu extended her hand. "And you are?"

"I don't want to tell you my name. I don't even know you. I came in here for a drink."

"I didn't mean to intrude." Blu could tell that she was getting nowhere with the woman. She stood up from the table and smiled at her. "You just seemed upset."

"Why wouldn't I be? After what happened today?"

"You're right. Especially if you knew Kirk. I'm sure it's heartbreaking."

"I'd never met him." She wiped at her eyes again. "Now I'll never get the chance to. Please, just let me have some peace."

"Blu?" AJ stepped up behind her. "I think she asked to be left alone."

"AJ, I was just trying to be friendly."

He quirked a brow at her and grasped her elbow with his palm. "Why don't you come talk to me for a minute?"

Blu allowed him to escort her back to the bar. Once

she was settled in front of her cheese fries she looked up at him. "Is there something wrong with talking?"

"Not unless the person has asked multiple times to be left alone. If that's the case, then you need to back off, or I end up getting complaints."

"I noticed her on the beach watching Kirk every single day. Do you know who she is?"

"I believe her name is Naomi, but anything more than that, I don't know. She must be a big fan—she asked me quite a few questions about Kirk."

"Did you notice any of the other contestants in the bar? Were they acting strange? I know that you had a hand in setting this whole thing up, so I'm curious about what you might have seen."

"No, Detective." He grinned.

"I'm serious." Blu bit down on a soggy cheese fry.

"No, I didn't notice anything odd about any of the contestants." AJ leaned against the bar. "Well, that one guy—Yale, I think is his name. He was in here a lot."

"Was he in here the night before the body was found?"

"Yeah, he was. In fact I had to escort him to his hotel. He had far more than a few too many."

"But you didn't see Kirk?"

AJ narrowed his eyes. "Actually, I did see Kirk. But not here. I saw him when I dropped Yale off at the hotel. Kirk was outside in front of the hotel. Yale started slurring words at him."

"What did Kirk do?"

"He just shook his head."

"Did he go inside?"

"No." AJ rubbed his chin. "It was like he was waiting for someone."

"I wonder who. He didn't seem like the friendly type."

"Maybe not, but a lot of people have a hard time being friendly." AJ smirked.

Blu glanced away. "I guess your uncle is running the backgrounds of all the competitors?"

"Of course. I don't think he suspects any of them, though."

"Why not?"

"Mainly because he feels it's a local job. See, only the locals would know that the beach would be unguarded at night, and none of the surveillance cameras from the bar point in exactly that direction."

"So?"

"So it would have taken quite some time to bury the body in the sand. In fact, they're not even sure yet how long it was there. But no matter when it was put in the sand, it would have taken a lot of digging. I don't think someone from out of town would risk getting caught."

"Do they have a cause of death yet?"

"There's no visible trauma." He paused a moment and met her eyes. "You enjoy really strange conversations."

Blu smiled and shrugged. "So no visible trauma? What does that mean?"

"Basically it means that he wasn't shot or stabbed. Nothing on the surface of the body explains how he died. So we'll have to wait for the internal exam and the results of the toxin screen."

"And do you think that the lab here can handle that?"

"What are you implying?" AJ raised his eyebrow.

"I'm just saying—maybe this type of crime would be handled better by more experienced—"

"You think we're just a bunch of uneducated beach bums, hm?"

Blu met his eyes. "I didn't mean it like that."

"Then how did you mean it?"

"I just meant that this is a very delicate situation and perhaps the police in the city would be able to handle it better."

"Well, darling, big city cops have no interest in small beach town murders, so I think it's safe to say that my uncle can handle it." AJ shook his head and turned away from her to stack some more glasses.

CHAPTER 13

"AJ, I didn't mean to upset you." Blu was quick to apologize the moment he turned away from her.

"Yeah, well, you did."

"I'm just worried that with this being a tourist town the first instinct is going to be to sweep it under the rug."

"Again, that's insulting. Have you ever looked up the word insult?" He turned back to look at her with a hint of frustration in the knit of his brow. "How can you judge someone so easily?"

"I don't mean to judge. I think maybe I should go."

"Yes, I think you should. I think you should go talk to my uncle about your suspicions and concerns. Then maybe you'll see he's not as incapable as you make him out to be."

"Fine." Blu stood up from the barstool. "But AJ, I really didn't mean that he was."

"Maybe you didn't mean it, but you sure think it. I can tell. Anyone who is from the big city comes in here acting like they own the beach and the rest of the world. For some reason I thought you were different."

"Maybe that's because I'm from a country town. I grew up far from the beach and far from the city, so I don't judge people based on where they live."

"Then what do you judge on?" AJ paused and looked at her.

"Mostly how people treat one another. I heard that you and your uncle were arguing on the beach earlier, and it's not the first time he's been short with you—I've seen that with my own eyes. I would assume that if someone can't even treat their own family with respect, then they probably have very little respect for people murdered in their town."

AJ smiled a little. "So you don't like him, because he doesn't respect me?"

Blu found herself caught in the question. If she denied it, she'd look like a liar, but if she admitted to it, she would reveal that she cared more for him than she should—considering that they barely knew one another.

"Maybe."

"Ha. That is not an answer." He flipped his towel up over his shoulder and narrowed his eyes as he peered at her. "One of these days you'll figure out that you can be honest with me, Blu. But until then you shouldn't judge my uncle too harshly. Maybe he has good reason not to respect me." He raised an eyebrow and turned away again.

For a moment all of Blu's focus shifted from the murder to AJ. What reason could his uncle have for not respecting him? AJ seemed like a pretty good guy. Maybe things had been different at another time.

Instead of waiting for AJ to turn back around, Blu left some cash on the bar and walked out. Since it was still early afternoon she headed for the police station. If AJ was right, and the police force was capable, maybe they'd have more details to tell her. Either way she thought they should be looking into the woman who appeared to be obsessed with Kirk.

When Blu arrived at the police station she found that it was empty. Not just empty of police officers, but empty of everyone. She stood in the lobby and looked around. At any moment she expected someone to step out of the bathroom or in from a side door.

The shrill ring of a lone phone filled the air. Blu shivered at the shock of it.

She noticed a picture of Kirk pinned up on a corkboard along with some other papers. After another quick look around she thought that it wouldn't hurt to take a quick look. Maybe she could get an idea of where they were at in the case.

She navigated her way through the desks to the corkboard. Once there she looked up at the photograph of Kirk. Luckily it was not a crime scene photograph but a picture of him beside one of his massive sculptures. She felt a twinge of disappointment that she'd never have the chance to see one of his creations in person.

When she tore her eyes away from the picture she noticed that there were several names affixed to the board. She could only assume that these were names of the current suspects. Yale was one of them, as was Bianca, and a few other contestants. There were also a few names that she didn't recognize.

Blu thought that they might be names of locals, or maybe some other people in Kirk's life that held a grudge against him. With his brusque nature it wasn't hard to believe that he likely had quite a few enemies.

Beneath each of the names was a list of information. Some were notes, some were photographs, or printed-off papers. From what she read there was very little to narrow down a specific suspect. She wondered if Yale might be top on their list, but there was nothing on the board that indicated that.

She reached up to look under one of the pieces of paper when a voice boomed right behind her.

"What do you think you're doing?"

Blu turned around quickly to find Chief Pitman's harsh glare fixed on her. She folded her hands behind her back as if she'd been caught by the principal.

"I was just looking."

"Looking at confidential information that is part of an active investigation?"

"Well, no one was here—"

"So you thought it would be perfectly fine to break the law?"

Blu squirmed under his dark stare. She wondered how Rachel would feel if she ended up locked up on her day off. She likely wouldn't have a job for long.

"I was just curious."

"Strange, the things that interest you."

"It doesn't seem like anyone is investigating the crime."

"That's a bit judgmental." He gestured to a chair at a desk. "Take a seat."

"It's okay, I'll just be on my way."

She started to move past him, but Chief Pitman moved between her and her way out.

"Sit down. It wasn't a suggestion."

Blu raised an eyebrow. "Are you charging me with something?"

"Should I? I could. Again, you were breaking the law when I walked in here."

"Is there really a law against looking at a corkboard?"

"Do you want to find out?" Chief Pitman rested his hand on the portion of his belt that his handcuffs dangled from.

Blu wasn't sure if it was intended to be a threat or just a habitual movement. Either way, she sat down in the chair.

"Good. Now why don't you tell me exactly why you're here?"

CHAPTER 14

Blu eyed Chief Pitman carefully. "I told you. I'm curious about the case." She braced herself for potentially being thrown out of the police station.

The police chief tilted his head to the side and seemed to be regarding her with a mixture of contempt and irritation.

"This isn't a sideshow, you know—not something to gossip with the other nannies about."

"That's not why I'm here. I thought maybe I could help."

"You? How could you possibly help?"

"I'm probably one of your best witnesses. I was at the beach every morning while the experts were preparing their areas."

"I'm sure anything you know, we already know."

"Do you know that there was an obsessed fan watching him every single day?"

"What?"

Blu smiled. "Her name is Naomi—that's all I know. But she was there every time I was there, before I got there, and after I left. She only ever watched Kirk."

"Well, that is interesting, but it doesn't make her a killer."

"How about Yale? Have you seen the videos that he posts online? They're full of hatred and threats against · Kirk."

"The investigation is still ongoing."

"So that would be a no, then?"

"Show me." He pointed to the computer.

Blu eyed him for a moment. There was something about him that made all of his intimidation tactics seem not so intense, and yet she was fully aware that he could easily toss her into a holding cell.

She leaned over and searched for Yale's videos. When they came up, Chief Pitman sat down heavily in the chair in front of the computer.

"Yes, there's some hatred there. Hm. Let's see if he's in the system."

He did his own search for Yale, but this time it was in the national criminal database.

"Aha, here he is." He pulled up a record. As he did a few other officers walked in.

"Chief, we need to talk to you." One of the officers gestured to him.

"Excuse me a moment." Chief Pitman stood up and walked over to the officers.

As soon as he was away from the computer Blu leaned forward to take a look at what he'd found. She could see that Yale's personal history was pulled up. In bold red writing she noticed the word assault.

She peeked over at Chief Pitman, who was still in the middle of a conversation with the officers. She reached out and grabbed the mouse. Then she clicked on the red word. It opened another window. In the window it detailed a previous arrest.

The perpetrator was accused of throwing a shoe at another individual. Perpetrator claimed that the actor's attempt at portraying one of his favorite characters was unsatisfactory and he only had a shoe available to throw. No bodily damage was caused but the victim pressed charges.

"A shoe?" Blu tried not to laugh.

"Snooping again?"

Blu jumped at the sound of Chief Pitman's voice. In her lifetime one of her strengths had always been observation. Chief Pitman seemed to have an almost supernatural ability to sneak up on her.

"You were busy."

"I thought you worked with kids?"

"I do."

"Yet you have no patience." He sat down in the chair again. "Well, a history of assault is damning, but the actual assault that took place was not exactly violent."

"Good point." Blu nodded. "What about Naomi?"

"It'll be hard to come up with anything off a first name only, but I'll see what I can do. In the meantime, Blu, I'd appreciate it if you would stay out of this. You think you're helping, but what you're really doing is running the risk of contaminating a criminal investigation. That is never acceptable."

"I'll be careful."

As she left the police station she was certain that she'd never be able to let the investigation go—not until the murderer was found.

The next day Blu woke to the chaos of the children running back and forth down the hallway. She checked her clock to see that it was just after six in the morning. They were up very early.

She pulled herself out of bed and headed into the hallway to see what they were up to. Just as she stepped out into the hallway Marley barreled past her on all fours.

"Meow!"

"Marley, shh, Mommy is sleeping."

Right behind her Joey charged forward on all fours as well.

"Ruff! Ruff ruff!"

"Shh, Joey!" Blu sighed. "Let's go, my little pets, and I'll get you both some breakfast."

The children happily paraded into the kitchen, still on all fours, but thankfully quieter.

She noticed that Rachel's bedroom door remained closed, though she doubted that the woman had slept through the commotion.

The kids could barely sit still long enough to eat their breakfast. They were ready for a day on the beach, but one glance at the television confirmed to Blu that the beach was still off limits. If the kids wanted to have a fun day, it would have to be elsewhere in town.

She thought about taking them to the park but the temperatures were hovering above ninety and she didn't think they would be able to enjoy themselves outside in the heat. Instead, she decided to take them to the mall a few miles away. It would be a nice change of pace and give Blu the opportunity to think things through.

"How about if we head to the mall today? They have that little train that you can ride on. And maybe your parents can meet us there for lunch. I bet your dad would enjoy that." Blu smiled as she herded the kids into the kitchen.

"Oh, didn't Mom tell you? Dad left early this morning. One of his business deals fell through and he has to see if he can fix it," Joey said.

"Oh no, I didn't realize that he'd left. I'm sorry."

Now she understood why the kids were up so early and also why Rachel had closed herself off in her room. Her heart ached for the woman who she knew was lonely without Marshall.

"Me too." Marley stuck out her bottom lip. "I wish he'd stayed."

"Don't worry, he'll be back soon." Blu stroked her hair. "Until then, we can have fun on the train. Hm?"

"Yes! Train, please!" Marley hopped up and down.

Joey toyed with his fingers and frowned. "I don't know if I want to go to the mall."

"We can see if they have any new video games." Blu grinned. She knew this always worked for Joey. Even if he didn't get to buy it at the time, he loved to see what was new and play on the demonstration machines for a little while.

As expected, his expression brightened. "Alright!" He jumped up.

"Go get dressed, kids."

CHAPTER 15

Blu took some time to prepare coffee for Rachel. She also made sure that the radio was set to Rachel's favorite music station so that the moment she turned it on she would hear something enjoyable.

None of this was part of her job description, but Blu cared for Rachel as much as she cared for Rachel's children. In many ways, she considered keeping the entire family happy to be part of her job.

Once the kids were dressed they headed out of the house.

Blu's mind raced with all the questions about the murder.

The mall had just opened when they arrived. She smiled at the security guard that opened the door for them.

"Early risers, huh?"

"Yes indeed."

"Most of the stores are still opening up but the arcade and the train are ready to run."

"Great!" Blu smiled.

She steered the kids away from the arcade, as she knew once they started to play she wouldn't be able to get them away from the games.

"Aren't you two lucky, you'll get the whole train to yourselves!"

"Come with us!" Marley tugged on Blu's shirt.

"No, sorry, I can't, sweetie, it's only for kids. But I'll be right here when you're done, okay?"

"Let's go, Marley, we can sit in the front and ring the bell!" Joey grabbed his sister's hand and tugged her onto the train.

Blu paid for their tickets. She waved to them as the train took off through the mall.

While they chugged off, Blu's senses were immersed in the smell of fresh coffee. She turned around to see that the small coffee shop a few feet away had opened. A cup of coffee sounded like the perfect way to pass the time before the kids returned.

As she stood in line to order it she noticed a familiar face in line ahead of her. It was Bianca, the other competitor in the sand sculpture contest.

"I just don't understand why they had to cancel the contest. They could have just moved it further down the beach."

The woman with Bianca frowned as she looked over at her. "Don't you think it would have been weird to continue to compete knowing that Kirk was dead? I mean they don't even know who killed him."

"Look, I get it that death is tragic, but this particular death wasn't all that tragic. I think people need to realize that Kirk is no great loss. In fact, the environment will probably benefit from the fact that he's gone. He was a polluter and he had no care for the animals or the environment. It was nearly impossible for me to work around his vibes, he was so toxic."

"Shh, Bianca, you shouldn't talk like that." Her friend cleared her throat. "You never know who might overhear you."

"I don't care who hears it. It's the truth."

"But what if his family or someone who cared about him heard you?"

"Cared about him? Are you kidding?"

"What do you mean?"

Blu did her best to act invisible. She was very curious about what Bianca had to say.

"Once my guru advised me that all of the hatred I carried for Kirk was clogging up my chakras. So, in the interest of keeping my energy flowing I decided to make an attempt to befriend him. I thought, how bad could he be, really?

"So I spent some time with him. I found out that he has no family, has barely ever had a girlfriend, and doesn't like animals or children. If that wasn't enough, he then informed me that he thought I was silly, flighty, and that I needed to consider that the earth would be destroyed by space matter long before the environment could kill us off—and that I was basically wasting my time by keeping my footprint as small as possible. When I tried to argue the point with him, he laughed in my face, called me a kook, and walked away."

"Wow." Bianca's friend paused to place their coffee order, then looked back at Bianca. "I can see why you had a hard time working with him. But still, I think you should consider keeping your thoughts to yourself. I'm sure the police are still looking for a suspect."

"Let them look. A guy like Kirk probably had plenty of enemies in his past. Once the truth comes out about him, I bet the police don't even bother looking that hard. The murder investigation will come up dry and his file will end up in a drawer somewhere. No big deal."

"I've heard rumors that maybe one of the other competitors did it. What do you think? What about the guy with the feathers?"

"Yale." Bianca snorted. "That man wouldn't have the strength to kill the bird those feathers came from. He's more interested in sand dyes and ribbons than he is in anything of substance. I don't know. Kirk has dominated the competition for so long that any number of competitors might be holding a grudge against him."

Blu listened so intently that she was potentially standing much too close to the two women, but neither appeared to notice.

CHAPTER 16

Bianca finally quieted down as she was handed her coffee. She turned with her full cup of coffee, but her eyes were still on her friend. Before Blu could take a step back to avoid her, Bianca walked right into her. The hot coffee splashed between them.

Blu grimaced as the liquid soaked through her thin blouse and singed her skin.

"Oh, watch it!" Bianca huffed. "I just bought this!"

Her friend grabbed napkins to help her mop herself up.

"You walked into me." Blu narrowed her eyes.

"Well, I didn't even know you were there."

Blu couldn't argue that point, as she had been doing her best not to be noticed. "I'm sorry. I can buy you another cup if you'd like."

"No, it's fine. I've got to go buy a new shirt, and now I'm not in the mood for coffee." She tossed the cup into the trash.

Blu stared at her. For all of the spouting off she'd

been doing about protecting the environment, it was hard to believe that Bianca would so casually toss a paper cup into the garbage instead of the recycling bin.

Her eyes met Bianca's. "You're one of the sand sculpture contestants, right?"

"One of the live ones—yes."

Blu accepted a napkin from Bianca's friend and offered her a smile of gratitude. "I'm sorry for your loss. It must have come as a shock to you."

"Sure. Whatever. Anyway, sorry about your shirt." She turned and walked away with her friend rushing behind her to catch up.

Blu sighed as she looked down at her shirt. She heard the kids' train returning in the distance. Joey and Marley would be back in a minute and there was no time to buy a new shirt—not that she'd want to pay mall prices, anyway.

"Here, I saw what happened." The young man behind the counter of the coffee shop slid her a cup of coffee. "On the house."

"Thanks." Blu smiled at him.

"Sometimes I wonder if some people are even human." He shook his head. "Did you hear the way she was talking about that dead guy? I didn't have a problem with him."

"You knew Kirk?"

"Not by name. He came here for a cup of coffee a few times. He was always polite. He even tipped me."

"Was he by himself?"

"All except for one time. He was with a woman."

"Maybe a girlfriend?"

"Oh wow, I hope not. She was angry. They sat at a table with their coffees and two minutes later she was screaming in his face."

"Really? Why? Did you hear anything?" Blu added some cream and sugar to her coffee while she nonchalantly questioned him further.

"Something about it not being his business—that it was too late, and that he needed to stay out of it. I figured it was some kind of personal issue. Then she knocked over her coffee and stormed out. Kirk even helped me clean it up and apologized."

Blu frowned. "Was she a young woman?"

"No, I'd say she was about his age. Maybe a year or two younger."

The train whistle drew her attention. "Thanks for the coffee. I gotta run."

"Sure, no problem." He smiled at her. "Might want to get a new shirt though."

"I will." She nodded.

As she collected the kids from the train they were so excited that they didn't even notice her shirt. Blu was so preoccupied with wondering who the woman with Kirk could have been that she forgot all about it.

As they left the mall Chief Pitman stepped inside through the same door.

"Excuse me." Blu backed away enough to give him room to get through the door.

"What happened to you?" He raised an eyebrow.

Blu was confused for a moment until she realized that he was looking at her shirt. She looked down to see that the spilled coffee had left a very embarrassing pattern.

"Coffee mishap." She cleared her throat. "Going home to change now."

"Wait, I'm here to speak to you."

"Me? How did you know I was here?"

"I spoke with Rachel and she told me that you took the kids to the mall. Hi there." He smiled at them. "Want to go play some games?" He reached into his pocket and pulled out a few quarters.

Before Blu could say a word, the kids grabbed the quarters and headed toward the arcade.

"Why are you looking for me?" Blu shifted from one foot to the other. Had he decided to charge her for nosing around at the police station?

"Because the toxin screen came in. Kirk was poisoned."

"Poisoned with what?"

"I don't even know the name of this stuff. According to the tech, it's used as a pesticide. He was injected with it."

Blu shuddered at the thought. "That's awful. So someone poisoned him and then buried him in the sand? Why would they risk bringing him back to the beach?"

"That's what I can't figure out. Not only was he murdered, but it's almost as if the killer wanted him to be found."

"Hm." Blu looked at him. "Why are you telling me all this?"

"You said you wanted to be part of the investigation."

"And you said that I should leave it alone."

"Well, that was before. Now I want you to tell me everything that you'd noticed while at the beach. Someone killed this man on my sand, and I can't let it go."

Blu was relieved by his determination. At least his focus was not to sweep things under the rug. "I'm afraid there's not much that I can tell you. I think that Kirk's biggest problem was that no one liked him."

"Most people don't like me either." Chief Pitman smirked. "That doesn't mean that they'll kill me. Someone had to hate him more than everyone else."

"There was a woman here with him the other day—at the coffee shop just inside. The clerk at the coffee shop was just telling me that they'd gotten into a pretty fierce argument. I thought that it was Naomi at first, but he said that the woman was Kirk's age."

"Naomi?"

"The woman with the hat and the sunglasses that I told you about. I thought you were looking into her?"

"I will." He frowned. "AJ tells me that you're pretty good at figuring these things out. Did you flunk out of the police academy or something?"

"No. But I did toy with being a journalist at one time. I guess I've just always been interested in the truth."

"That's a commendable way to be. It can also be dangerous." He met her eyes. "We're dealing with a ruthless and cunning person here. Just be careful what you get yourself into."

"You'll let me know if you find anything out about Naomi?"

"Sure. I'm going to meet with security and see if I can figure out who Kirk had an argument with as well. If you think of anything else that you might have seen or overheard, please contact me."

"I will."

"Blu, come play a game with me!" Joey called to her from the arcade.

"Looks like you're needed." Chief Pitman laughed.

"Always." Blu grinned.

She walked over to the kids and joined Joey in a game of Pac-Man. The bright lights and the music did nothing to block out the roar of thoughts that flickered through her mind.

Who would have poisoned Kirk?

CHAPTER 17

Rachel was waiting for them in the front yard when they arrived home. As Blu parked in the driveway she walked over to them with a bright smile.

"Morning, everyone. Were you off on an adventure already?"

"We rode the train!" Marley wrapped her arms around Rachel's legs.

"Oh, how nice." Rachel looked at Blu with warmth in her eyes. "I appreciated the coffee and the music this morning."

Blu nodded and laughed as Joey rushed past her to take his mother's hand.

"I beat Blu at Pac-Man! Chief Pitman gave us some quarters to play."

"Oh, that's nice, sweetie." Rachel waited until Joey chased after his sister, then she looked at Blu. "When Chief Pitman asked me where you were—I'm not going to lie—I was a little concerned. What's going on? Anything I can help you with?"

"Oh, no. He was there to speak to me about what I might have seen at the beach."

"Oh? Were you able to help?"

"Not much, I'm afraid. I just wish they would get the case solved so that the kids could get back to enjoying their summer on the beach."

"Well, it's probably for the best that you didn't see too much. The kids don't even seem to be aware of what's going on."

Blu nodded. Then she met Rachel's eyes. "I'm sorry that Marshall had to take off so soon."

"Me too. I know to expect it, but I have hard time accepting it."

"Hopefully soon he can be around more often."

"I hope so. Anyway, I thought I'd take the kids out to lunch. Would you like to join us?"

"I think I might stay home if you don't mind."

"No problem. I thought you might want to, since they got you up so early this morning."

"Yes, I could use a little nap." Blu laughed.

"I'm sure. We'll be back after lunch." Rachel ushered the kids right back out the door.

Blu sent them off with a wave.

She closed the door and savored the silence. After working with kids for so many years she didn't really notice the noise level—until it was gone. Then the silence sounded like the loudest thing she'd ever heard. She let the peace wash over her senses, but even as her body began to relax, she had no desire to take a nap.

What she wanted, instead, was to dig deep into the murder. She wanted to find out if anyone had seen anything suspicious in the hours before the morning of the murder.

When she was a journalism student she'd learned a few tricks to get large amounts of information from people in a local area. Social media was usually the best bet.

She did a search for community groups for the local area. As soon as she found one with a large amount of members she joined it. After being automatically approved, she began sifting through the posts and comments from the day before the murder until the current date.

There were many complaints about the local bakery's inability to make a decent cake. There were several posts about items for sale, as well as rants about the tourists on the beach. Her head began to swim as she read through so many posts.

Then she came across one that held her attention. It was regarding a late-night driver. The person who'd posted about it described bright headlights driving through town at around three in the morning. When the driver had turned on to the road that led to the beach, the lights had shone right through the person's bedroom window, waking them up. It wasn't much, but it did place activity near the murder scene around the time of the murder.

Blu wrote down the person's name who'd made the post—Robin Carter. She did a search for Robin's name and found a local address. With a quick glance at her watch, she figured she had about an hour before Rachel and the kids would be back from lunch. She grabbed her keys and hurried out to her car.

As she opened the car door her cell phone began to ring. She pulled it out of her purse.

"Hello?" She juggled the phone against her ear as she climbed into her car.

"Hey, Blu."

It took her a moment to realize that it was AJ. "AJ, what's going on?"

"I just wanted to touch base with you. I'm getting together with my uncle later to discuss the case. I need this settled. I want my bar and my beach back."

"Is that an invitation?"

"Actually it's a request. My uncle said he had some information that he wanted to share with you. So can we meet later?"

Blu glanced at her watch. "Well, I'm doing something right now, and I'll probably have the kids later. Maybe we could meet at the park?"

"Sounds good. What are you up to?"

"Uh." Blu glanced at the address on the seat beside her. "Just running some errands."

AJ cleared his throat as if he might have sensed that

she was holding something back. "Alright, so around two?"

"Sure. I'll see you then." Blu hung up the phone and backed out of the driveway. She wanted to make sure she had plenty of time to talk to Robin.

It wasn't until she arrived at Robin's house that she realized she had no idea what she was going to say to the woman. She wasn't a police officer—or even a local. She was a stranger asking a bunch of questions.

Blu searched her mind for any ideas that might make the woman more comfortable with talking to her. She tucked in her shirt, smoothed back her hair, and did her best to look professional.

She parked in front of Robin's house and strode up the driveway with purpose.

CHAPTER 18

When Blu reached the front door she straightened her shoulders and knocked three times, then stepped back. A moment later the door swung open.

A woman, whom Blu judged to be about in her forties, stared out through the screen door at Blu.

"Can I help you?"

"Are you Robin Carter?"

"Why?"

"Ms. Carter, my name is Donna Cash. I'm here to talk to you about your recent complaint."

"Complaint?" She shook her head. "I think you have the wrong person."

"I don't think so, Ms. Carter. One of your neighbors saw your complaint on the Internet and reported it to my department. I'm just here to confirm the details."

"I didn't agree to make any report. What is this about? What department are you from?"

"Public Works. Actually, it's a division of the Public Works department. My division deals with keeping the beach residents protected from the influx of tourists. Yes, we do need the revenue from tourism but our local residents are still entitled to a sense of safety and peace. From what I understand you had that sense of peace violated recently."

"Is this about the headlights?"

"Yes. There's no reason for someone to be out that late."

"It wasn't just the late hour. It was that the lights continued to shine through the window for so long."

"About how long? Do you remember?"

"At least five minutes, maybe ten."

"So the car was stopped?"

"I guess."

"Which window is your bedroom window?"

Robin stepped out through the screen door and pointed to the window at the side of the house that faced the beach. "I'm used to the flickering of lights going by from people coming back from the beach, but this was more than that. I needed to get to work early the next day. I mean, I was mad about it then, but I don't really care now. I don't want to cause any trouble."

"It's important to report these things, Ms. Carter. If no one does, then it just gets worse and worse. Now, did you by any chance look out the window? Did you see the car?"

"Well, the headlights were bright, you know. So I couldn't see too much."

"But did you see anything at all?"

"It looked like it was a dark color. And maybe one of those SUV types. I couldn't see the back of it, so I guess it could have been a truck. I'm not sure."

"How about the driver? Did you get any glimpse of the driver?"

"Look, what good is any of this going to do? Even if I did see a face, it was probably a tourist that's long gone. What's the point of all of this?"

"One voice can make a difference, Ms. Carter. I'd just like to know if there was anything else that you noticed? Did you see the vehicle leave?"

"I almost didn't. After the headlights were turned off, I started to go to sleep."

"Wait, turned off?"

"Yes. After about ten minutes the headlights cut off. I figured whoever it was had found whatever address they were looking for. So I tried to go back to sleep. Just as I was falling asleep I heard the car drive past. I wouldn't have noticed it otherwise."

"Why not?"

"The driver never turned the headlights back on."

"That's strange."

"Very. I don't know how they were able to stay on the road without being able to see."

"Thanks for the information. Any other little detail you might have noticed would help a lot."

"I told you everything I know. Like I said, I don't want to get involved. It was a one-time thing."

"Thanks again. I'll be in touch if I have any more questions."

Robin nodded.

Blu walked back toward her car. She checked her watch again. She had maybe a half hour before Rachel would be back.

When she started the car, instead of turning around, she drove the path that the mystery car would have taken. She did so very slowly. When she reached the beach she turned her car around and backed the car up. Then she turned on her headlights. She could see the glimmer of them on the very window that Robin had pointed out.

Blu turned off the engine and the headlights. Then she stepped out of the car. The Beach Bum parking lot was a few feet away. The beach itself was mere footsteps away. She could see the crime scene tape flapping in the wind where the body had been buried.

It was clear that if the driver had backed the vehicle up to the sand, it would have been very easy to then drag the body to the spot where it had been found. Blu's best guess was that the vehicle was some kind of SUV, which would have given the killer plenty of room to store and move the body.

She started to walk toward the spot marked with the tape, but her phone buzzed before she got halfway across the sand. She checked it to see that Rachel had sent her a text.

We're home. I'd like to go out for a massage if you can be back soon?

Blu texted back.

Be there in five minutes.

She tucked her phone back into her pocket. With one last look at the crime scene, she tried to focus her mind back on her real job.

When she opened her car door she noticed something on the ground. When she looked closer she could see that it was a feather—a dark blue decorative feather.

CHAPTER 19

Blu's heartbeat quickened. She started to reach down to pick up the feather, then happened to think that touching it might be contaminating evidence. She leaned into the backseat of her car and pulled out a leftover disposable cup. She put the cup over the feather and dug it down further into the sand.

Then she sent a text to AJ.

I found something on the beach that your uncle should check out. I put a red cup over it in the sand.

Just in case AJ and the chief didn't follow through, she snapped a picture for her own records.

As Blu started her car she looked once more in the direction of Robin's house. There was no way to know for sure how long the car sat in front of the beach, but Blu imagined it couldn't have been more than fifteen to twenty minutes.

There was no way someone could dig a hole and bury a body in that short amount of time. She was fairly certain that whoever had committed the crime had dug the hole at the beach first. This would have meant that the crime had been planned in detail.

Her stomach churned with disgust. She couldn't fathom a mind that would piece together such a cruel act.

When Blu arrived at the house, the kids were just finishing a television show.

"Sorry I'm late, Rachel."

Rachel grabbed her purse and smiled at her. "No problem. We had a nice time. Now I need to relax a bit."

"Have fun." Blu walked into the living room to join the kids. "Hey guys, you wanna to go to the park?"

"No beach?" Joey frowned.

"Not just yet, kiddo. But the park is just as good, right?"

"Not really."

"You love the swings."

"Good point." Joey grinned.

"Alright, we're going to just go for a bit, then we'll have the rest of the afternoon to play some video games, okay?"

"Yes!" Joey raced to get his shoes on.

Blu helped Marley into her sneakers, then they headed out the door.

She checked her phone but still hadn't received a text back from AJ. She had no idea if the feather had been collected or not. She was tempted to go back and collect it herself, but the kids were too excited to go to the park.

As they headed for the car in the driveway, a man walked toward them from the street. Blu tensed, as she didn't recognize the man. She was highly protective of the children.

"You're Blu, right?" He paused a few feet away from her and the children. He wiggled his fingers at the kids in a friendly way.

Blu placed an arm around the children to keep them from walking further.

"I'm sorry, we're just leaving."

"I can see that. I need to ask you a quick question. It will only take a minute."

"What is it?"

"I'm Kirk's manager."

"I'm sorry for your loss."

"Thank you. I tried to get some information out of the local authorities but they weren't very forthcoming. So I tried to do a little investigating of my own, and to my surprise I discovered that someone had beat me to it. Your name kept coming up."

"Oh? Kids, why don't you go ahead and get in the car?"

Joey opened the door for Marley.

Blu looked back at the man in front of her. "So you know my name, but I don't know yours?"

"Frederick."

"Frederick, I'm just a nanny as you can see. I'm not sure what I can tell you."

"Or what you're willing to share?" He moved closer to her. "I can't get a word out of the police, but you—I thought might be more reasonable. Kirk had a lot of fans and they're demanding answers. I can't exactly move on without knowing what happened."

"Were you and Kirk friends?"

"No one was friends with Kirk."

"Someone was. I heard that the night before he died, he was waiting for someone outside his hotel."

"Who told you that?"

"Who was he waiting for? Was it you?"

Frederick narrowed his eyes. "You're quite clever, aren't you, Nanny Blu?"

"I don't know. But I do know that you're the only person who has shown up here interested in Kirk. Yet you claim not to be his friend. So you must be getting something out of this."

"I'm going to lose a lot of money. I had tons of contests and appearances booked for Kirk. Now that he's dead, I have to figure out what to do about those appearances. I can turn them into a memorial, honoring his memory, and likely make twice the money—but that won't go down well unless the murderer is in custody. As it stands now—the way his body was found—people will be turned off by it."

"Well, that's a good reason to care." Blu shook her head. "Was this guy really as bad as everyone makes him out to be?"

Frederick sighed. "He wasn't a bad man—he just wasn't quite human. Or maybe he had some kind of mental or emotional challenge. He cared more about his sand than he did about anyone else on the face of this earth."

"I'm sorry. I don't think I can help you."

"Can't or won't?"

"I think you need to go back and try to speak to Chief Pitman again. I'm sure if there's anything that he thinks you need to know, he'll fill you in."

"I bet." He studied her for another moment. "I'll be in touch, Blu."

She watched as he walked away. The blare of the car horn made her jump.

"Joey! Get in the back seat!" She hurried to the car.

CHAPTER 20

The drive to the playground was filled with squabbling that Blu barely noticed. The arrival of Frederick had turned another wheel in her mind. He had confirmed that no one liked Kirk.

But then there was Naomi. Naomi, whom she still knew nothing about.

The kids hopped out of the car as soon as she parked.

"Go ahead and play. I'm just going to make a quick phone call."

"You're it!" Joey tagged Marley on the top of her head. Marley lunged after him.

Blu checked her phone yet again to see if she'd gotten a text back from AJ. There was still nothing. She flipped through to the picture of the feather. As she stared at it she heard the crunch of gravel from behind her.

"Hey there, Blu."

She looked up at AJ. "Hi yourself. Did you get my text?"

"Yes."

"Did you go get the feather?"

"Yes, that was a clever way to keep it contained."

"I think it might be one of Yale's."

"That's possible, or it could be anyone else's."

"Right." She was about to tell him about the headlights and the early morning beach visitor, but before she could Chief Pitman pulled up. He walked over to the two of them.

"Not hunting any more feathers, Blu?" He winked at her.

"Did you hear from Frederick?"

"The manager? Yes. He was quite an interesting fellow."

"What about Naomi?"

"Alright, take it easy there. I did a search on her, but I couldn't find any information. I checked the local hotels and motels and they didn't have anyone with a first name Naomi registered. I don't have a last name to go on."

"We need to find out who she is." Blu snapped her fingers. "I'm sure she's connected to this somehow."

"What did I tell you, AJ? We should just get her a badge."

"Take it easy on her, Uncle Paul, she's just trying to help."

"I am." Blu looked at the chief. "I want to know that the beach is safe for the kids to play on."

"That's my job, remember?" Chief Pitman raised an eyebrow.

"I do remember. But if I'm able to speed things

along, that's great. Summer only lasts so long, you know."

"Well, so far we still have nothing to go on."

"Then we need to do something to change that." Blu narrowed her eyes with determination. "I know! Let's have a party."

"What?" AJ looked at her.

"That seems terribly inappropriate." Chief Pitman shook his head.

"A celebration of life—a way to honor Kirk. If Naomi is the fan she claims to be, then she'll resurface and we'll be able to find out who she is. Besides, there's no better way to find out the truth than by getting a group of people together with a little food and alcohol. I'm sure that Frederick will show, as well as Bianca and Yale."

"That's ridiculous." Chief Pitman shook his head. "That's not how we do things."

AJ tilted his head from side to side. "She's not wrong, Uncle Paul. I know far more than I want to know about anyone in this town."

"So we can scatter some officers in the bar—in plain clothes—to listen in on the conversations and see if anything useful comes up."

"But nothing they overhear will be evidence."

Blu said, "Maybe not, but it might give you some direction. Right now we're no closer to figuring out who killed Kirk than we were the day his body was found. Don't you think we need to change that?"

"Sure we do, Nanny Detective, but that doesn't mean

that we can just throw a party."

"Why not?" AJ shrugged. "She can use the bar. Just about everyone who was in town for the competition is still here, even the contestants. I think it's a good idea."

"Thanks, AJ." Blu flashed a smile at him.

He smiled back.

Chief Pitman rolled his eyes. "Alright, you can have your party, and I'll even send a few officers to attend, but if anything gets out of hand we're going to shut it down. The thing that neither of you appear to be thinking about is that we don't know if this killer is done. It's pretty easy to inject someone with poison. How do we know getting everyone together won't inspire the killer to knock off someone else?"

"I guess we'll just have to be very careful." AJ frowned. "I'll make sure the security cameras are working well."

"Do you think we could pull it off by tomorrow night?" Blu glanced over at the kids, who still played on the playground. "Rachel might let me have a few hours off tomorrow to arrange the party."

"I say we give it a shot." AJ shrugged. "Let me know what you need from me, and we'll go for it. I'm sure Shawna would help waitress."

"No." Chief Pitman spoke up sharply.

AJ looked over at him.

"I don't want Shawna anywhere near that bar, understand?"

"Sure." AJ nodded. "It was a stupid idea."

Chief Pitman straightened his collar. "I have to go. Keep me up-to-date on the progress of the party. Alright?"

"Sure." AJ watched as the older man walked away.

"You okay?" Blu studied his tense expression.

"Why wouldn't I be?"

"It just seemed like maybe there was an issue there about Shawna."

AJ locked eyes with her. "Investigate the murder, Blu, not me." He winked at her, then walked off in the other direction.

Blu sighed. She sat down on a swing beside Joey.

"Are you going to try to touch the sky, Blu?" Joey grinned and stretched his legs out as he swung upward.

Blu followed his movement and looked up at the sky. It was a beautiful day, but she had barely noticed. The kids always had a way of reminding her to slow down.

She swung beside Joey for some time and enjoyed the sound of Marley's laughter as she chased the birds.

CHAPTER 21

On the way back from the park Blu focused her thoughts on the SUV that had been parked near the beach. Someone had to be driving it, and that someone was likely the killer. Instead of trying to find out who killed Kirk, maybe she needed to find out who had been driving the SUV.

The kids were more than happy to be home after such a busy day.

"Blu can we have popcorn and watch a movie?"

"Sure, Joey. Just give me a minute to put my things down."

"I get to pick the movie!" Joey shouted as he ran for the living room.

"No, me!" Marley chased after him.

Blu paused at the table near the door and set down her purse and keys. As soon as she set down her keys, it hit her. She had just promised both the chief of police and AJ that she'd be able to throw together a memorial party within twenty-four hours. What was she thinking? How could she possibly accomplish that?

Her heart raced and her breath came short. She dug her phone out of her purse and called the only person that she knew was likely to help her—no matter how crazy her plan was.

"Hi, Blu, what's up?" Maddie's voice was more cheerful than she'd expected.

"Maddie, I need your help."

"Help with what?"

"I need to put together a memorial party for Kirk by tomorrow night."

"Huh? Like maybe candles on the beach?"

"No. Like, a party at the Beach Bum with every person who could possibly know Kirk and plenty of people that don't. I'm not sure that I can pull it off, but I know that I definitely can't do it without you. Do you think you can help?"

"I can absolutely help. You know I love a challenge! This is just like one of those reality television shows where the woman has to throw together a perfect wedding in a day, only this is a memorial, so I guess it's not really like that, but you know what I mean."

Blu closed her eyes for a moment. "Yes, I know, Maddie. How soon can you be here?"

"The kids are out with their mom right now, so I can be right over."

"Thank you, Maddie. You're a life saver." She hung up and headed into the living room.

Once the movie was chosen and started she popped

some popcorn for the kids.

While she waited for Maddie to arrive, Blu decided to investigate the one detail that she hadn't revealed to Chief Pitman or AJ. If the person who killed Kirk was one of the contestants, or in town for the contest, then they would likely have rented a vehicle. Most of the people that came into town did.

If the person decided to rent a car, they probably didn't keep it long—maybe for a few hours, maybe for a day. She opened up the phone book and grabbed her phone. She found three car rental places in the area. She punched in the number for the first rental place.

"Hi, I was wondering if you could tell me what cars you've rented in the past three days—specifically whether you rented any vehicles to one of the people in the contest that was taking place at the beach?"

"I'm afraid we only do weekly rentals, so I'd have to go back a little further."

"No thanks, I appreciate your time." Blu hung up and dialed the next car rental place.

"Hello, I was wondering if you could give me an idea of how many cars you may have rented over this past week."

"Sure. We rented—looks like forty-two."

"Wow, that's a lot."

"We're running a special."

"Do you by any chance have any discounts on daily or hourly rates?"

"Actually, yes, we do. We have a half-off special on twenty-four hour rentals."

"Have you rented any in the past three days with that special?"

"Ten."

"Were any of those cars rented to one of the contestants in the sand sculpture contest?"

"No, I'm afraid not."

"What about to a Naomi?"

"Last name?"

"Sorry, I only have the first name."

"Naomi, Naomi." He mumbled for a moment. "Nope, sorry."

"Is there any way that you could e-mail me a list of the people who rented cars at the daily rate?"

"I guess. What's this about?"

"I'm just curious."

"Huh. Well, I'll tell you what—when Chief Pitman comes in and requests the list, that's when I'll e-mail it."

Blu sighed and hung up the phone. She knew she wasn't going to get any further with the guy. She called the last rental place on the list.

"Hello, Speedy Cars."

"Hi, I was wondering if you rent SUVs?"

"Yes, we specialize in them."

"Do you have any specials running currently?"

"We have a same-day rental discount. If you rent the car and return it on the same day, you'll be able to get the discount."

"What if I rented the car from an evening until a morning?"

"Yes, as long as you pick up the car at the end of the day and return it first thing in the morning the discount will still apply."

"Have you rented any SUVs out lately?"

"Yes, three. Why?"

"I'm just curious. I was riding with a friend of mine, and they had an SUV from a rental place. I'd like to rent one as well, but the vehicle was so clean and tidy that I want to rent one from the same place. I haven't been able to get through to her to find out the name of the company, so I was hoping that you might be able to tell me."

"Do you know the date that she rented the vehicle?"

"Yes." Blu gave the woman the date of the evening before the murder.

"Actually, we only had one evening rental that day. So it could possibly be your friend. Is her name Bianca?"

Blu's heart skipped a beat. "Yes. Yes, that's her name."

"Well, then it was her. Can I set you up with a rental?"

"Could I rent the same vehicle?"

"Unfortunately it's being cleaned. We detail all of our vehicles between rentals."

Blu frowned. She knew that if the rental place did a

thorough cleaning, then there was a good chance that all of the evidence had already been washed away.

"Let me give you a call back when I'm ready, okay?"

"Sure. Please ask for me—the name's Janine. We get a commission."

"Absolutely." Blu hung up the phone. "Bianca." She didn't have more time to think about what she'd just found out before there was a knock at the door.

"Hello? Blu?"

"Come on in, Maddie!"

CHAPTER 22

A moment later Maddie entered the house with a wide grin on her face. "You are going to love me!"

Blu was still dazed by the revelation of the person who was likely driving the SUV. She glanced at Maddie. "Hm?"

"Look what I have!" Maddie sat a big bag down on the table between them. It was filled with feathers, ribbons, and other decorative materials.

"Where did you get all that?"

"You know that guy Yale—one of the contestants? Well, I was driving past one of the hotels and saw him lugging this big bag of decorations toward the dumpster. So I stopped and asked if I could have it. He said that since there wasn't a contest he was getting rid of these things and he didn't care who took them. So, voila! We can use some for decorations for the party."

"Wait a minute. Don't even open the bag."

"What? Why?"

"It might be evidence."

"Evidence of what?"

"I'm not sure yet." Blu paced back and forth. "I discovered some information that points to Bianca as the killer."

"Bianca? Isn't she the one that's all into peace and love?"

"Maybe that only counts for the people that she likes."

"Blu, how far are you getting into this case? Should I be worried about you?"

"The point of the party is to draw out the killer."

"Wow." Maddie sat down hard on one of the kitchen chairs. "That sounds dangerously exciting."

"I don't know how exciting it is, but I want to find out the truth."

"So what do we need to do?"

"We need to get the word out about the memorial. We also need to make sure that there are enough eyes and ears there to keep track of all of the suspects. AJ will keep the alcohol flowing. It's time we got the truth out of someone."

"What if no one cops to it?"

"Well, I have a few leads."

"Have you talked to Chief Pitman about them?"

"I haven't. I'm not sure if I should just yet."

"Why?"

"The thing is that the police want to rush in and put an end to this. I'm just a little concerned that the goal is more to close the case than to find the real killer. Right now I have some proof that might implicate Bianca. But something doesn't sit right with me about that. I did also find a feather close to the crime scene that I think may have belonged to Yale."

"Okay, I'll start posting on the local sites and the sand sculpture contest site about the memorial. I'll also put some calls out to the most talkative nannies about it. Don't worry, Blu, getting the word out is not going to be the problem. The problem is going to be getting people to talk. Most murderers aren't too chatty."

"Some are." Blu frowned. "I know it's a stretch but it's the only thing I can think to do. Chief Pitman isn't going to haul anyone in for questioning without some kind of evidence. So we need to bring the questioning to the Beach Bum."

"It's a plan." Maddie shrugged.

The two women spent the next few hours making calls and preparing for the party. When Maddie left for the night, she promised to meet up with Blu at Marley and Joey's early morning horseback riding lesson. It was a short summer class, but the kids—especially Marley—enjoyed it.

After Blu tucked the kids into bed, Rachel arrived home just in time to say good night.

"I got caught up in some things after the massage." She frowned.

"Rachel, is everything okay?"

"I guess. The town is in uproar over the murder, which I understand, but some people are just rude."

"What happened?"

"I was going to pick up a few things at the grocery store but when I tried to get through the door these two men were arguing in front of it. Neither of them would budge."

"Did you know them?"

"No. I think one of them was one of the contestants from the contest, but I'm not sure."

"What did he look like?"

"To be honest, it was hard to see past all of his strange make-up."

"Ah. Yale." Blu narrowed her eyes. "Any idea who he was arguing with?"

"He kept calling the guy Frankie. No, that wasn't it. Freddy, I think it was Freddy."

Blu's eyes widened. What in the world would Frederick and Yale have to talk about? "I'm sorry that happened."

"Well, it's over now. I'll just go to the grocery store tomorrow. There's no way I was going to get in the middle of that."

"I can stop at the store in the morning after the kids' riding lessons if you'd like. Just leave me a list on the kitchen table."

"Thanks." She smiled. "What would I ever do without you?"

Blu smiled in return. She hoped that she'd never need to find out. Although she did her best not to play favorites, working for Rachel and Marshall had been her most enjoyable job so far.

CHAPTER 23

Blu walked down the hall to her bedroom and closed the door behind her. As soon as she sat down at her desk she opened up her computer. She began to type up a story that was forming in her mind. It was easy to pin the murder on Bianca—she was an angry woman, who tended to rub people the wrong way.

Yale obviously hated Kirk more than anyone else in his life.

Alone, neither of the suspects made sense to her, but when she combined Yale with Frederick it made perfect sense. Frederick wanted to get rid of Kirk and make a new star. Yale was on board for being that new star. They concocted a plan to take out not only Kirk, but Bianca as well, by using her name on the car rental.

It sure looked like they could have been setting Bianca up to be framed for the murder—she didn't doubt that Frederick had the knowledge to pull it off. If she went to Chief Pitman with the information she had, she might be playing right into the plan.

A large yawn reminded her of how exhausted she

was. She gave in to the need to sleep, but her mind did not. She lay awake for hours with thoughts about the killer playing through her mind.

The next morning Blu woke early, despite not having slept much at all. She made a pot of coffee to perk herself up and prepared a quick breakfast for the kids. For once, she was the one who had to wake them up.

"Let's go, we have your riding lesson today!"

Both of the children bounded out of their beds and fought each other to get into the bathroom.

Blu grinned as she refereed the fight. She still hadn't figured out how she was going to plan the memorial and set it up while having the kids at her side for most of the day.

On the way to the riding lesson she still debated whether she should tell Chief Pitman about the SUV or the fact that Bianca's name was on the rental agreement. She decided that she'd rather speak to Bianca first. Maybe armed with the knowledge that she had she could rattle the woman into making a confession.

Once they were situated at the riding lesson, Marley ran up to the small pony that served as her magnificent steed. "Ready to ride?" She giggled.

Joey was helped up onto his horse.

Blu snapped a few pictures, then watched as their teacher led them off down a path through the woods.

"Blu!"

Blu jumped and turned around to see Maddie a few feet away.

"See, I told you I'd be here."

"Where are the kids?"

"Skate party. It's some kind of thing that goes all night. They have my number if they need me."

"That sounds like fun."

"I hope so. It's hard to find things that they both enjoy these days. So what's up? Did you talk to AJ yet?"

"AJ? No."

"Oh, I just figured you'd want to share your information with him."

"Not just yet."

"Well, I made sure that I got in contact with everyone I could about the memorial. I assume AJ is providing drinks and food?"

"Yes."

"Okay, then we should be all set. Unless you want to put up some flyers?" She produced a stack of papers with a smile. "How much do you love me?"

"More than you could ever know!" Blu hugged her, then took the flyers. "The kids and I will have fun putting these up today. That should get us a big crowd."

"I just hope it works out the way that you want it to."

"Me too."

"Well, I'll get a head start on putting some of these out now. If anything comes up call me. Otherwise, I'll meet you at the Beach Bum tonight."

"Okay. Thanks again, Maddie."

"Just remember me when you collect the reward money." She winked, then walked away.

Blu tucked the stack of papers under her arm and watched as Joey and Marley made their way back out of the woods. For Marley it was just a fun ride, but Joey seemed to have a real passion for his horse. He always took a little extra time after the lesson to brush and care for the horse. That kind of passion spoke of a love for animals.

It was the same kind of love that Bianca expressed for the environment. Blu couldn't help the thought that appeared out of nowhere.

At the grocery store there was a special on quite a few items. Blu was careful to keep both kids close as she maneuvered the aisles in search of the items on Rachel's list. Between checking the list and the labels, and wrangling two children who wanted everything they saw, Blu didn't notice when someone reached past her to grab the last pack of frozen chicken breast.

It wasn't until Joey tried to toss a box of donuts into the cart that Blu looked up, and right into Bianca's eyes. The thought of the kids being so close to someone who might be a killer caused Blu's heart to jump in her chest.

"Joey, over here—now!" She pointed to the side of

the cart.

Joey protested, but lined up with the cart.

"Oh, it's you." Bianca smiled. "Is there something in the grocery store that you're planning to spill on me?"

"No." Blu took a slow breath. She needed to get her wits about her if she was going to attempt to find out the truth about Bianca.

"Oh, good. Now if you don't mind, you're standing right in front of the bacon."

"Chicken and bacon?" Blu raised an eyebrow.

"Hm? So?" Bianca tossed the items into her cart.

"I don't know, I guess that I just assumed that you'd be vegan."

"You shouldn't assume things about me. I can be quite surprising. If you notice, I only buy organic free-range meat that has been humanely harvested. I do believe that our bodies require meat for sustenance; however, I can't support the torture of animals."

"What do you mean torture?" Joey looked up at her.

"Oh, sweetheart, haven't you ever seen how your chicken nuggets are made?"

Blu covered Joey's ears and glared at Bianca. "Please don't. He's not old enough."

"Sure, sure, just let him wallow in his ignorance so that he can grow up to be yet another corporate puppet. I'm sure you're doing a great job of molding a good little soldier."

"Odd choices for a hotel room." Blu tilted her head

toward the meat in a cart, choosing to ignore the comments about Joey.

"Oh, I'm not staying in a hotel. I have a friend who lives on a houseboat. She's letting me share her space. Although I guess by tomorrow I'll be leaving."

"Leaving?"

"Sure. The contest is canceled—no real reason for me to stick around."

"Aren't you curious about what happened to Kirk?"

"Not really. He got what was coming to him. Why do I need to know more than that?"

"Has your friend been driving you around?"

"What do you care?"

"I just thought I saw you. In an SUV?"

"Trust me, you didn't see me in any SUV. Now if you don't mind, I need to finish my shopping." She walked off exuding all the confidence in the world.

But was it the confidence of a criminal about to get away with a murder? That was the real question Blu was asking herself as Bianca walked away.

CHAPTER 24

With a little bit of arranging, Blu was able to get the evening off. She didn't ask for it often, so Rachel was usually very flexible when she did. She'd said that she understood why Blu would want to go to the memorial.

When Blu arrived at the Beach Bum, AJ was just setting up for the party.

"Hey, Blu, I think we're going to be crowded."

"Really? Are you going to have enough help?"

"It would be better if Shawna was here, but you saw how that went down with my uncle."

"Does your uncle really have that much say?"

AJ raised an eyebrow.

Blu anticipated that he might actually share something with her, but he only returned to straightening out the tables.

"Is there anything I can do to help you get ready?"

"You could wipe the tables off if you want."

Blu grabbed a towel and the cleaner and began spraying and wiping off the tables. The entire time she felt her anxiety build. Would the memorial be a complete waste? Would anyone even show up? Kirk wasn't well-liked. Maybe people couldn't be bothered to attend.

Not even ten minutes later, Blu's concern was alleviated.

People began arriving in droves.

Blu scanned the faces of the people in the crowd. Most were either locals or summer people. She noticed quite a few of the nannies that she was familiar with.

She didn't, however, see Naomi.

When the bar door swung open she looked toward it. Maddie stepped inside and waved to her. She weaved her way through the crowd.

"I can't believe that you put this together so fast!"

"I didn't really do much. You and AJ did everything. Can you do one more favor for me, Maddie?"

"Sure, what is it?"

"See that guy over there?" Blu pointed to Yale.

"Oh yeah, the crazy guy."

"He's not crazy. He's creative." Blu grinned. "Can you maybe shadow him a bit, see what he's talking about?"

"No problem." Maddie grinned. "I feel so detective-y."

"Just don't get too close. We do need to be careful since we don't actually have any idea who the killer might be."

"Oh, I can be subtle." Maddie tugged at the collar of

her sleeveless shirt and smiled. "When I want to be."

Blu hoped that she was right. The last thing she needed was any chaos.

As the night went on she began to lose hope that Naomi would show up.

A loud clinking sound drew her attention to the center of the room. Bianca stood on the top of one of the small tables.

AJ started to walk around the side of the bar. Before he could reach Bianca, Blu placed a hand against his taut chest. "Please, let's see what she's going to say?"

AJ lingered there for a moment, his eyes on hers. "If she gets hurt, it's my fault, you know?"

"Don't worry. I'm sure she knows exactly what she's doing." Blu crossed her arms, then turned back to look at Bianca.

"Now I know that we're all here tonight because of Kirk's tragic death, but I think it's time to be honest about it. It was *not* that tragic."

"Hear, hear!" Yale lifted his glass high into the air. "Good riddance to bad rubbish."

A flutter of whispers carried through the room in reaction to his words.

Bianca cleared her throat. "There are some people in this world that are only here to poison it. Kirk was one of those people. I'm not here to drink to his life, I'm here to drink to his death."

A shocked silence filled the bar. One of the waitresses

cranked up the music.

AJ grabbed Bianca around the waist and easily lifted her down from the table. "One more act like that and I'm going to have to kick you out."

"I'm so scared." Bianca rolled her eyes. "Bring me another vodka, bartender."

AJ glowered at her, then he looked over at Blu.

Blu could see from the curve of his hands and the clench of his jaw that he wanted to toss Bianca out of the bar. She shook her head at him.

AJ grimaced and turned back to the bar to get the drink. Blu knew that if Bianca was thrown out she'd lose her chance to get a drunken confession from her.

Maddie walked up to Blu and sighed. "All I'm hearing is his boasting about his video views. I'm not getting anything out of him. How about I talk to him directly?"

"You'd be okay with that?" Blu searched her eyes.

"Sure I would. My talkative nature is one of my special skills." She smiled.

"Alright, but be careful. If he does anything to make you uncomfortable let me or AJ know."

"I will."

CHAPTER 25

Blu watched from afar as Maddie fluffed her hair. Then she walked right over to Yale. She sat down beside him and leaned close. Yale fixed her with a withering stare, but a moment later he laughed. Then he leaned closer to Maddie.

Blu shook her head in amazement. "How does she do that?"

"It's called being friendly." AJ grinned. "Remember, I suggested that you should try it sometime?"

Just as Blu was about to come to her own defense with AJ, she heard the door swing open. She saw a woman pull off her hat and sunglasses. She already had a tissue clutched in her hand. There was no doubt in Blu's mind that this was Naomi. She turned away before the woman could recognize her, as she didn't want to spook her.

"Very funny. Now let's see how friendly you can be to Naomi."

"Huh?"

"I don't think my charms are going to cut it. So your job is to see what you can get out of her." Blu gestured in Naomi's direction.

"Are you handing out assignments now?" AJ met her eyes.

"Are you going to do it or not?" Blu tightened her lips.

"Alright, alright. I'm going." He tossed down his towel and picked up a bottle of wine. He walked toward Naomi's table.

Blu looked over at Maddie to check on her, then she glanced back in time to see AJ lean down close to Naomi's ear. She couldn't hear what he was saying but whatever it was made Naomi giggle.

She pointed to the chair across from her. AJ slid into it and opened the bottle of wine. He poured a glass for Naomi first, then for himself.

As they chatted, Blu could see the way AJ held her gaze and smiled in a seductive manner. It was surprising to her that he was so very good at this. It occurred to her that he had to be to make good tips.

When Naomi reached out and stroked the back of AJ's hand, Blu felt her stomach twist. A quick heat rose up in her cheeks. She looked away as fast as she could. What was going on? Why did she care who touched AJ?

When she looked back she saw that Naomi was alone at the table again.

AJ spoke up from a few inches to the side of her. "I

have to get back to the bar. All I managed to find out was that she collects starfish and she dreams of having kids."

"That's an interesting combination. All of that and no last name?"

"Nope, sorry. I got the impression that she didn't want to tell me anything."

"Hm. Interesting. Why would Kirk's biggest fan be so evasive about who she is?"

"Sorry I couldn't be more help."

"That's alright. I have other ways of finding out."

"Why does that frighten me?" AJ lifted an eyebrow and smiled.

"It should." Blu grinned.

As she walked away from him she wondered if he was watching her. It made her stomach flutter at the possibility. Why? She had never had any difficulty with ignoring a man, whether he was making advances or not, but somehow AJ seemed to be twisting her up inside.

She did her best to focus on getting close to Naomi without her noticing. She waited until a waitress came by to ask if she'd like anything to eat. While Naomi spoke to her, Blu jumped at her chance.

She slipped in behind Naomi and carefully picked up the glass. Then she slid it into the plastic bag she'd pulled out of her purse. She carried it over to the bar, where AJ was trying to handle several orders at once.

"I have something I need you to get to your uncle."

"Give me a second." AJ whipped a few drinks

together.

Blu took a moment to admire his skill behind the bar. He could flip and toss things with incredible dexterity. When he was finished he delivered the drinks. Then he turned to look at Blu. "What is it?"

"This is Naomi's glass. I'm hoping he can get fingerprints off it. Maybe we can find out who she really is."

"Alright." He set the glass on the back of the bar. "I'll get it to him as soon as the memorial is over. How are things going out there?"

"I think Maddie has Yale under control." Blu tilted her head toward the couple. Maddie was nearly in his lap, and Yale summoned more drinks for the both of them.

When Blu turned back to AJ he shook his head.

"The woman has her talents."

"What's that supposed to mean?"

"Nothing." He turned away from the bar to make a few more drinks.

Blu decided to try her own charm out on Frederick. He was sitting at a table with a few of the locals. They seemed to be quite interested in his stories of fame and fortune.

"So I told her—look, just because you're a movie star, that doesn't mean that I'm going to bow down and do whatever you want. I'm not that type of manager."

"Shoot, I would have bowed down and did anything she asked." A burly man with a toothy grin chuckled and slapped the table.

"Maybe, but if you do that they'll never respect you. These famous types—they want servants."

MACI GRANT

CHAPTER 26

Blu sat down beside Frederick. "Is that what Kirk wanted?"

"Oh, you again." He smiled at Blu. "I thought I might be seeing you again."

Blu didn't miss the less than subtle wink Frederick sent toward the other guys as they seemed to take it as their cue to leave the two alone at the table.

"Did you have any luck with Chief Pitman?"

"I didn't even bother. A small-potatoes police chief like that isn't going to get to the bottom of this."

"Or maybe that's what you're hoping for. You've gone from representing starlets to managing a sand sculptor? That's a pretty big change."

"There were some misunderstandings." Frederick picked up his mug of beer and took a long swallow.

"I bet. Maybe you miss that life—with all the fame and glamour. Maybe you thought Kirk could be your way to get your name in the newspaper again. Nothing like a good scandal to attract the attention of the Hollywood types."

"Interesting." He set his mug back down. "So your perspective on this is that I killed my own client?"

"All I'm saying is that there was no emotional connection between you and Kirk. Maybe you decided that it would be worth it to sacrifice him so that you could create a great tragedy around his life and his death—maybe even get some big documentary out of the whole thing."

"You're nuts. I had nothing to do with Kirk's death."

"Correct me if I'm wrong, but wouldn't it be normal for a client to expect that his manager was going to be there on the day of his big event? Only you weren't even in town, were you? Did you have a more important client, or were you just trying to give yourself an alibi for the time of Kirk's death?"

"You think you're really clever, don't you?" His eyes darkened as he leaned across the table toward Blu. "Are you completely clueless about what making false accusations can lead to?"

Blu met his eyes that were glaring at her now. "I'm not easily intimidated."

"Maybe you should be." He slid a hand across the table, the intensity of his glare increasing; he didn't look away for even one second. "Because I'm not the type of man to toy with. Do you understand me?"

Just as Blu opened her mouth to respond she felt two hands come down on her shoulders. A ripple of tension carried through her body as a quick fear rose within her.

A moment later she heard AJ's voice.

"Is there a problem here, Blu?"

"No problem." Frederick smirked. "I was just leaving. I've had enough of this place." He stood up and tossed a few folded bills on the table. "Keep what I said in mind, Blu. If you mess with a shark, you're going to get bitten."

"Is that so?" AJ's hands tightened on her shoulders. "I might not know much about sharks, but I can tell you this—if you mess with her, you're not going to have any teeth left."

Frederick sneered and walked away from the table.

Blu shrugged off AJ's hands and then followed him as he started walking away. "Thanks for that, but I was handling it."

"Maybe you were, but the man needs to know where his boundaries are."

"And you think it's your job to set those for me?"

AJ's gaze locked with hers. Blu noticed a flicker of something before he looked away. "Don't get all defensive. I don't let any man mess with any woman in my bar. It's bad for business."

Blu bit into the tip of her tongue. Had she assumed too much?

"I need to close up soon."

"Really? I haven't even gotten anything to work with."

"Sorry, Blu, I have to follow the law. I can't serve alcohol past a certain hour."

"So we did all of this for nothing?"

"Maybe if we sleep on it something will come to us. Besides, I have the glass to give to my uncle, right?"

"Right." Blu nodded.

She and Maddie helped AJ tidy up the bar.

When it was time to leave Maddie grabbed her arm. "Do you need a ride home?"

"No, I have my car."

"Okay." She hugged Blu. "Sorry we didn't crack the case."

"That's okay. Thanks for all your help."

As Maddie walked out Blu stepped behind the bar to grab her purse. When she turned back around AJ was waiting for her.

"I'll walk you out to your car."

"Thanks."

The parking lot was dark aside from one bright street lamp positioned closer to the street. It reminded Blu of the headlights that Robin had seen.

They were almost to Blu's car when raised voices drew her attention. Not far off, closer to the beach, Frederick and Yale seemed to be arguing. AJ started to move toward them to break them up, but Blu put a hand on his forearm to stop him.

"Let them have it out."

"If they start throwing punches I'm ending it."

"Fine." Blu nodded.

She moved a little closer so that she could hear what

they were saying.

"I didn't point her toward you! I didn't point anyone toward anyone. Tomorrow afternoon I'm leaving this town, and I can promise you I'll never be back." Yale was shouting slurred words at Frederick.

"You know as well as I do that the contest comes here every year."

"Well, I won't be."

"Are you giving it up?"

"I don't know. After this, I'm just not sure I can do it any more."

"Are you nuts? You can't quit now!"

"I can do whatever I please. Kirk gave his whole life to this. He had other things he could have done, but this was all he did. Now he's gone. It's over. He never even righted his wrongs. Do you think that's what I want to happen to me?"

"Don't be ridiculous. Kirk was murdered. Who would want to murder you?"

"I can think of a few people."

"Promise me you'll think about it, Yale. You're drunk. Don't make any rash decisions."

"Maybe I need to be drunk. Maybe I need to stop thinking about him being buried in the sand."

"You hated him. You didn't hide it."

"Yes, I hated him, but I didn't want to see him dead."

"So you say."

"I mean it. I was in my hotel all night until I left for

the contest in the morning."

"Likely story."

Yale shook his head. "I'm done. I'll never sculpt another sandcastle."

"We'll see." Frederick shrugged and walked past him.

Blu frowned as she paused by her car. "Interesting."

"Don't worry, there's a cab to take him back to the hotel," AJ said.

"That's not what I mean. I mean it's interesting that Yale is ready to quit. Why would he kill Kirk and then quit the contests all together?"

"Maybe he didn't plan on killing Kirk. Maybe it just happened."

"No way. It had to be preplanned. Someone went to the beach and dug that hole. Someone picked the beach as a burial place. This has ritual written all over it."

AJ leaned against her car door and met her eyes. "You constantly surprise me, you know that, Nanny Blu?"

"Why?" Blu brushed her hair back from her eyes and tucked it behind her ear. She noticed that AJ's large frame was blocking her from getting into her car.

"Because. You act like this perfect nanny—this soft, gentle, loving person around the kids, but now—here you are talking about murder like it's just another item on your grocery list."

Blu narrowed her eyes. "You know something, AJ?"

"Hm?"

She pushed a hand against his thick shoulder until he

moved away from her door. "I can't ever tell if you're trying to pay me a compliment or insult me."

Blu opened the car door, but before she could slide in, AJ's hand caught her by the elbow. The heat of his touch was something that she couldn't compare to a sunny day or a warm bath—it was something much deeper than that, as if he was the temperature of passion itself.

"It's always a compliment, Blu. Always." He offered her a small smile, then released her elbow and walked away.

CHAPTER 27

Blu tried to get her heart to slow down as she settled into the driver's seat. She rubbed her elbow where AJ had touched it, not because it hurt, but because she expected his presence to remain there somehow. She saw him glance back at her from the door of the Beach Bum; then he disappeared. If only she could get her heart to stop pounding she might be able to figure out what had just happened. She took a deep breath and drove toward the beach house.

As she drove she tried to focus on the case, not on any strange emotions she felt for AJ. In the morning she knew that she was going to have to tell Chief Pitman what she'd discovered. It made her uneasy to think about the lingering doubts she still had about the person she was getting ready to accuse. But with everyone leaving, an arrest had to be made, even if it was just a guess.

The next morning she lied to Rachel. It was becoming a nasty habit. She told her that she had an appointment that she'd forgotten about. Rachel agreed to keep the kids for an hour.

Blu arrived at the police station with a heaviness in her heart. She was ready to reveal what she'd found to Chief Pitman, but she still wasn't certain if Bianca was the right suspect. When she walked into the police station she noticed that AJ stood beside his uncle at one of the small desks. They were both leaning over a computer screen.

Blu took another breath and reminded herself to not lose her mind yet again if AJ happened to accidentally touch her.

She walked up to the two men. "Good morning."

"Ah, Blu—just who I wanted to see." Chief Pitman swung the computer screen around so that she could see it.

Blu focused on the screen instead of AJ's eyes, which seemed to be focused on her.

"Is that Naomi?" the chief asked.

"Yes. Did you find out who she is?"

"Thanks to your hard work, yes I did." Chief Pitman tapped the screen lightly with his fingertip. "This young lady was telling us all quite a few lies."

"Oh?" Blu felt a sense of relief. "Is she the killer?"

"Well, we're not sure about that yet. But we do know why she was hanging out around Kirk."

"Why?"

"Kirk was her father."

"What?"

"It's true." AJ moved a little closer to her. "When

Uncle Paul ran the fingerprints from the glass they came up in the system—not for a crime, but because she'd added her information to a missing persons bank in the hopes of being reunited with her father one day."

"Oh wow." Blu sunk down into the chair in front of the desk. "That poor girl. She never even had the chance to talk to him."

"Maybe it was for the best, considering that he wasn't the greatest guy in the world."

"No, it couldn't possibly be for the best." Blu shook her head. "Everyone deserves to have the chance to know who their parent is. I mean—if that's what they want."

"Her parent was the man who raised her." AJ crossed his arms.

Blu glanced up at him. From the tension in his brow she assumed she'd hit a nerve.

"Anyway, regardless of the tragedy of the situation, this discovery also led us to another connection. One of the shop managers at the mall was able to identify the woman from the surveillance video as Naomi's mother."

"They must have been arguing about him meeting his daughter." Blu shook her head. "That means that he knew Naomi was here and that she was looking for him. But he didn't even bother to talk to her?"

"Some men don't want to be fathers."

"AJ." Chief Pitman looked across the top of Blu's head at him. "I think that's enough."

Blu braced herself for AJ's usual mouthy response.

Instead he only nodded.

"Okay, so maybe Naomi and her mother had something to do with all this?" Blu glanced back at the chief.

"Maybe." Chief Pitman shrugged. "But either way we're not going to find out anything more until we interview them. Unfortunately we have to find them first."

"It just doesn't make sense. Naomi's mother didn't want Kirk around Naomi. Kirk apparently wasn't interested in Naomi. That might be enough to send Naomi—a grieving, rejected daughter—over the edge, but would her mother really help? Why would they take him out in an SUV in the middle of the night to bury him in the sand?"

"What did you say? An SUV?" The chief's head snapped up at her words.

CHAPTER 28

Blu took a deep breath as Chief Pitman and AJ both focused their attention on her. "Oh, I was getting to that. I might have found a witness who might have seen a black SUV in the area of the crime scene around the time of the murder."

"And you didn't lead with that?" Chief Pitman leaned closer to her. "We *might* have been able to find the car and who the renter was! We might have been processing that information as we speak!"

Blu wheeled her chair back a few feet to avoid spittle. "I actually already did all of that. But there isn't going to be any evidence to find because the car has been detailed."

"Unbelievable. Then who rented the SUV?"

Blu bit into her bottom lip. She looked between the two men, who were hanging on her every word.

"I thought maybe it wasn't her—that she was being framed."

"Tell me who rented the car." Chief Pitman scowled

at her.

She felt her heart drop, wondering how much trouble she'd be in if she withheld information.

"It was Bianca."

"You know this for sure?"

"The clerk confirmed it."

"How did you get a hold of someone so fast?"

"Well, I…" Blu looked over at AJ, whose grimace communicated that she was about to face Chief Pitman's wrath. "I might have found out yesterday."

"Yesterday?" The chief's voice roared through the police station.

Everyone stopped what they were doing, and a stunned silence stretched throughout the building.

"You knew about this yesterday? Did you know about this?" Chief Pitman swung his attention to AJ.

"No, I didn't." AJ frowned. "She didn't tell me any of this."

"So you just thought that you'd conduct your own investigation and fill me in when you felt like it?" Chief Pitman's voice lowered but his demeanor didn't change. Everyone began to get back to their work but it was still much quieter than it had been.

"I just didn't think it was valid information. I thought maybe Frederick and Yale were working together to frame Bianca."

"Too many soap operas, hm?"

"Sir, I didn't mean to cause a problem. I just wanted

to be sure before I accused anyone of murder."

"You know what we do here, Blu?" He sat down on the edge of the desk and looked into her eyes. "We investigate crime. We don't just go around pointing fingers at people and hollering murderer! Do you see any pitchforks hanging on the wall?"

Blu lowered her eyes. "I'm sorry. I guess I didn't really think it through."

"If we had that information yesterday, we could have questioned Bianca yesterday. Do you know how valuable time is during an investigation?"

"I'm sorry."

"Do I look like your boss?" He raised an eyebrow.

"Uncle Paul, she apologized." AJ started to move closer to Blu.

"You stay out of this. I told you to keep an eye on her. Obviously you didn't." He looked back at Blu. "I don't need your apologies. I'm not your boss, your parent, or even your friend. What I need you to do is get out of my police station, and I promise you that if I end up with nothing in this case, I'm going to make sure that you and your employers are not welcome back in this town. Do you understand me?"

Blu stared up at him. The misery she felt inside blossomed into something else. "I haven't done anything wrong. I haven't done anything for you to hold it against Rachel and Marshall."

"I decide that, not you. Now get out." He pointed to

the door. "AJ, make sure she gets to her car."

AJ frowned. "Uncle Paul, be reasonable—"

"Don't start, boy." Chief Pitman shot him a scathing glare.

AJ sighed and curled a hand around Blu's shoulder.

Blu was shocked at the way AJ acquiesced so easily to his uncle. For all of his muscles, his temper, and his smart mouth, he acted like a scolded child as he led her out of the police station.

"Wow, I'm going to file a complaint. How dare he be so rude to me? And to threaten the family that I work for?" Blu sputtered out her words as AJ walked her to her car. "That man is on a serious power trip."

AJ jerked her car door open and met her eyes. "Or maybe you should have trusted him enough to give him the information when you found it."

"You're taking his side?"

"There are no sides here, Blu. Sure, Uncle Paul has a temper, but he's also under a lot of pressure. He wants to solve this murder as much as you do. More, since—you know—it's his job."

"AJ, if I thought it was important—"

"That wasn't for you to decide." AJ kept his voice low but his tone had a bite to it. "Anyway, just stay out of it, alright? Uncle Paul will calm down. He's not going to talk to Rachel or Marshall. Just stay out of his way."

"I can't believe that you think this is okay."

"Look, Blu, I get why you're upset. But my uncle

doesn't tell anyone anything. He trusted you with the information about Naomi, and you're just a nanny."

"Right." Blu furrowed a brow at him. "I forgot. I'm just the summer help."

"I didn't mean it that way."

Blu shook her head and shooed him away from her car. She slammed her car door shut and started the engine. AJ still stood beside the car when she rolled the window down.

"I guess I'm supposed to take that as a compliment too."

He stared after her as she drove away.

Blu couldn't resist a glance in the rearview mirror.

CHAPTER 29

When Blu arrived at the beach house, Rachel was ready to head out.

"Thanks again, Rachel."

"No problem. I forget things too." She smiled at Blu.

Right after Rachel left, the sky opened up with rain. Blu had hoped that she'd be able to lug the kids around town to continue her investigation, but now that wasn't a possibility—not that it mattered, since she was now on Chief Pitman's bad side. She toyed with the idea of making a few calls but she wasn't even sure whom to call.

When her cell phone rang she saw that it was AJ. She almost sent it to voicemail, but at the last second she picked it up.

"Hello?"

"Hey, Blu. Don't hang up."

"I'm not."

"Good. I just want to let you know that Uncle Paul brought Bianca in for questioning."

"Did he arrest her?"

"Unfortunately no. He didn't have solid enough

evidence to hold her."

"So he just let her go? She's going to fly home today!"

"There's nothing he can do. His hands are tied."

"Well, mine aren't."

"Blu, don't. I talked him down this morning but he's not the kind of man that you should aggravate."

"Listen, AJ, you might be scared of your uncle but I'm not."

"No, Blu, listen to me—"

Blu hung up the phone. She wasn't about to be told what to do. She was furious that they would let a murderer escape. Kirk would never have his justice. So what if Chief Pitman was upset with her? He didn't have any control over what she did. She was a private citizen after all, and if she wanted to investigate, then she could investigate.

She snatched up her phone and dialed Maddie's number.

"What are you doing?" Blu blurted out before Maddie could even speak.

"Ugh—trying not to lose my mind with this weather. The kids are crawling the walls."

"So maybe adding two more to the mix might not be a good idea?"

"Huh, why?"

"I just want to check something out and I think it would be best to do so without the kids."

"Sure, you can bring them over if you want. I'm going

to pop popcorn and make it a movie day."

"You're sure the kids won't mind?"

"Please, if either of them looks up from their tablet and notices I'll be shocked."

"Okay." Blu laughed. "Thanks, Maddie."

"Anything for you, darling."

Her playful accent made Blu smile. Maddie always had a way of cutting through her stress and reminding her that life was supposed to be fun.

"I'll be over in a few minutes, then."

"Sounds good."

After Blu hung up she hurried the kids into their rain gear. She felt a pang of guilt. She knew that Rachel and Marshall paid her to watch the kids, not to leave them with someone else. But she couldn't risk Bianca getting away with Kirk's murder. That had to be good enough reason for slacking off on her duties for a few hours.

Once she dropped the kids off with Maddie, she drove toward the marina. The rain was coming down in sheets. Bianca had said that she was staying with a friend on a houseboat. Luckily for Blu, there were only a few houseboats in the marina. It wasn't a popular choice in the wealthy area.

She parked her car and stepped out into the pouring rain. For a moment she considered calling AJ for backup. But after their tense conversation earlier she thought that might not be the best idea. She was just going to see if Bianca was there. If she wasn't, then she might snoop around a bit. If she was, then maybe they'd just have a friendly conversation.

As she walked down the dock she noticed that there was a light on in one of the houseboats. She walked toward it as casually as she could. Just as she reached it a woman walked out. Blu recognized her as the one who'd been with Bianca at the mall. She quickly ducked back behind a post, looking away so the woman wouldn't recognize her.

"—and all I'm saying, Bianca, is that I don't like cops. You need to be out of here by tomorrow, got me?" She stalked past Blu without even looking in her direction.

Blu waited until she was sure that the woman was a safe distance away. Then she climbed onto the boat. Her heart raced the moment her foot touched the wet wood. She knew that this would be considered breaking and entering, but she was already on the boat. There was no turning back now.

She moved toward the door. It opened before she could reach for it.

Bianca froze in the doorway. "You? Why are you here?"

"I just want to talk to you for a minute."

"Right. For some reason you're trying to ruin my life. Do you have an explanation for that?"

"I'm just trying to figure out why your name was on an SUV rental."

"Uh, because I rented an SUV." She rolled her eyes.

"You? But aren't they bad for the environment?"

"Everyone has to slip up now and then." She shrugged.

"Could I come in? The weather is crazy."

"Why would I let you in?"

"Because I'm soaking wet and I just want to dry off for a second before I walk back to my car."

"Better reason." Bianca glared at her.

"Because I know that you're the one who killed Kirk and I have the evidence to prove it."

"Sure. That's why the police let me go."

"I'm not the police."

Bianca pursed her lips. She stepped aside to allow her in. "What is this, are you trying to blackmail me?"

"No. I just want the truth."

"Well, I didn't kill anyone, so there's your truth."

"If you didn't kill Kirk then why did you rent the SUV?"

"To go for a moonlit drive with my friends. That's all."

"Why would you be out so late on the night before the big contest?"

"Let me tell you a secret about these big contests. They're not that big of a deal. I only do them to raise awareness about the environment."

"So it must have bugged you that Yale used all of those dyes and things in the sand."

"Yale? No. He only used organic stuff. I helped him

with that. Kirk was the one that was polluting the beach."

"How?"

"That powder that he used in the sand. It was a pesticide. He was so stuck up that he didn't want a single bug in his sand. I mean, one ant can destroy quite a bit of work, but that's no excuse for poisoning the sand."

"Wow, I didn't know that was what he was using."

"No one did. I saw the powder once, and I tried to tell someone, but no one wanted to listen. Kirk was their golden boy."

"That had to make you angry."

"So what's this evidence you claim you have?"

"I have the syringe that you used to poison Kirk." Blu held her breath. She knew that she was taking a huge risk with her statement.

"No way. I didn't do anything like that."

"But it has your fingerprints."

"It doesn't."

"How can you be sure?"

"Because I didn't kill him."

A sudden burst of wind caused the boat to shift from side to side. Blu lost her footing, as her shoes were soaking wet. As she tumbled toward the other side of the boat, she saw a few syringes roll across the floor.

CHAPTER 30

While Blu was still trying to get upright, she saw Bianca pick up one of the syringes.

In the next moment the woman's arm was tight around Blu's waist.

"Just another nanny, washed away by the storm—nothing to have a memorial for." Bianca whispered. "Let's see if you have any proof after this."

Blu felt the tip of the syringe sink through the material of her sleeve. She took a deep breath as if somehow that might protect her from the poison.

The door of the houseboat burst open. It startled Bianca enough that she drew her hand back from Blu's arm, but she didn't release her grip around her waist.

AJ, rain-soaked and red-faced, filled the doorway. "Put the syringe down, Bianca."

"No! If you take one step toward me, she's as dead as Kirk."

Blu squeezed her eyes shut to keep from crying. She tried to think of a way to escape.

"Bianca, you're going to prison either way. Do you hear that?" AJ said.

Sirens rose above the sound of the rain.

"No way. I saw the way you looked at her last night. You're not going to let me harm a hair on her head, are you? I'm just going to walk out of here before your buddies can get to me."

Blu noticed the boat starting to lurch. She heard the roar of the wind. When she opened her eyes she caught AJ's gaze. She stared at him hard.

"Why did you do it, Bianca? Just tell me that. I have to know." Blu asked.

"What does it matter?" Bianca snarled. "The man was poisoning the sand. Sea turtles lay their eggs in that sand! He would have killed them all. For what? Because he's a star? No! He didn't deserve to live. He had to die. I killed him, and I gave him back to Mother Nature to do with what she would. She is the only force I answer to."

Blu took a deep breath as the boat rocked again. "Well, it looks like Mother Nature is pissed!" She shoved her feet hard against the floor in the same moment that the boat lurched to one side.

The force of her movement knocked Bianca off balance. She, the syringe, and Blu slid across the floor to AJ's feet.

AJ grabbed Bianca by the shoulders and hefted the slender woman up off the floor.

"Blu? Are you okay?"

Blu stared at the wood grain of the floor.

"AJ, what's going on?" Chief Pitman burst through the door.

"We've got her, Uncle Paul." AJ handed Bianca over to Chief Pitman. "I'm willing to bet you'll find syringes filled with the same poison in here. I also have her confession."

"What's wrong with her?" Chief Pitman tilted his head toward Blu.

"Blu?" AJ crouched down beside her, and picked up the syringe that was lying on the floor. "Blu, no! We need an ambulance! Uncle Paul, right now!"

AJ pulled Blu up into his arms.

She looked into his eyes. "AJ."

"Shh, Blu, it's okay. It's okay, I've got you."

"I'm okay."

"Shh."

"No. I mean, I'm okay." Blu opened her eyes wider. "I think I had the wind knocked out of me."

"She didn't stick you?"

"I don't think so."

"That's not good enough. Let the paramedics check you out. Blu, what were you thinking?"

"I was thinking that someone had to care about Kirk."

AJ brushed her wet hair away from her eyes and sighed. "I knew you were going to be more trouble than you looked."

"Is that a compliment?" Blu smiled a little as the paramedics rushed to her side.

"With you, it's always a compliment." AJ smiled as he held her close.

Blu's heart raced, not from fear—or even from excitement—but from being cradled in AJ's arms. She heard the commotion of the officers around her, the rush of the wind as it rocked the boat, but none of it could compare to just how loud her heart was beating.

It made no sense to her that he had such an effect on her, but for just once, she didn't try to figure it out. Instead, she rested her head against his chest and closed her eyes.

The paramedics looked her over from head to toe, checking her vitals. "No evidence of injury. Her heart rate is elevated, but that's to be expected."

Blu looked up into AJ's eyes. Maybe they expected it, but she certainly didn't.

ALL TITLES BY MACI GRANT

http://Amazon.com/author/macigrant
*Check the author page for current list of titles

Summer in Diamond Bay

#1 Lifeguards and Liars
#2 Sandcastles and Secrets
#3 Ice Cream and Intrigue
#4 Hot Dogs and Homicide
#5 Clambakes and Chaos

www.ingramcontent.com/pod-product-compliance
Lightning Source LLC
Chambersburg PA
CBHW070548180626
46817CB00005B/1746